REGRESSIVE

THE CULT OF SERENDEE

ANGEL LAWSON

FOREWORD

Quick note friends about warnings for Regressive.

There's some rough stuff in this book. The darkness is following poor Imogene but she's not the only one with demons. Anex is a cult leader. She and her guys are followers of the cult, trying to make their way though. Hopefully.

T/W: Dub-con, self-harm, knife and blood play, eating/food control, sex-trafficking, drug use/sales, cult behavior, captivity, forced branding.

Be safe, friends!

Angel

Make sure you follow my group, Angel's Antics on Facebook for all the good stuff!

ANGEL'S ANTICS

READER GROUP

1

I mogene

"It's too late, Imogene," he mutters low enough that only I can hear. "Welcome to the family."

Those are the words that haunt me as I watch Rex undress.

The last forty-eight hours have been complicated—confusing—he'd threatened to leave Serendee for good. He'd asked me to go with him. But in the end, we'd both stayed, our bond to one another witnessed by the entire community and most of all, his father.

Elon, Silas and Levi... they'd supported me, but none of it eases my nerves at seeing Rex shrugging his shirt over his broad, muscular shoulders. The last time we were together like this he hurt me—forced his way inside. Rex had claimed me in the physical sense, and I let him because that's how I was raised, what Anex Ordered. And now that he's my Bonded Mate, I'll do whatever he demands, despite the potential for pain.

Pain, I suspect, that will run deeper than the feel of him inside of me.

Methodically, he drapes his shirt over the back of a chair. The Mating quilt gifted to us by the women of Serendee lies smooth and crisp on top of the mattress. I wrap my arms around my waist, desperately trying to ground myself.

This is The Way.

This is what Anex wants.

This is what *I* want.

I repeat the words like a mantra, willing myself to accept them. I'm not afraid of sex. Not anymore. Silas showed me how good it can feel. But we'd left him, Elon and Levi after the ceremony, and I followed Rex back to our suite in the main house. Rex isn't Silas, a man trained to please women with the barest of touches. Rex is a brute. He's angry. Vindictive. And if it wasn't for me—and some strange obligation—he'd be gone from this world for good.

Rex saved me from something tonight, something I'm not even sure I understand, and for that, I owe him.

"Take off your clothes," he says, voice adrift. He faces away from me and when he drops his pants, I see the hard-curved lines of his backside. He's molded of marble. Like all gods should be.

My fingers move to the long row of buttons that travels my sternum, up to my throat. We'd made this agreement. I do what he asks of me—*everything* he asks of me. No questions. No arguments. My hands shake as they fuss with the buttons, and he finally turns, frowning when he sees my struggle.

"Christ," he mutters, coming at me. I stare at his erection, swollen and swinging between his legs. My belly drops, sparking that confusing mix of arousal and fear. His fingers replace mine, pushing at the buttonholes, the tattoo on his forearm shifting as his muscles unfurling as he works. "They make these fucking things like this just to make us crazy," he says, jaw tensing in annoyance. I shiver when the pads of his fingertips brush against my skin. "You realize my father's wives don't wear this type of clothing. He doesn't have the patience."

Irritation flickers in his cool blue eyes, and he grabs the fabric with both hands and wrenches them apart. The sound of tearing fills the room followed by the ping of buttons falling across the hardwoods follows. It took me months to create this dress, sewing each stitch by hand, fastidiously placing every button. In one furious moment he destroyed it—*ruined* it.

I look up at Rex's angry face. I absorb his chiseled jaw, the bright halo of hair, the mean darkness in his eyes. It's in all of these that I see him—the real him. All shreds of the decent man that came to my side at the Ceremony have vanished.

Good, I understand *this* Rex better.

He hurts. He takes. He controls. All I have to do is survive.

He pushes the dress off my shoulders, allowing it to pool at my feet, while his finger runs under the strap of my bra—one Elon bought me—and he tugs that, too, until my breasts break free. His fingers ghost around my nipple—toying, teasing—until he tweaks it, forcing a cry from my lips.

He grins and says, "I love that sound, Little Lamb," scooping me up and tossing me on the bed. Not bothering with the covers, he climbs over me, his weapon sharp and pointed between his legs.

I've barely caught my breath, settled my eyes on his intimidating frame when he spreads my legs and presses the tip of his cock against my entrance. My fingers wrap in the quilt, bracing myself for the impact, but he just hovers there, eyes meeting mine.

"You're still taking the contraceptive?" he asks.

I blink, trying to process the words. Contraceptive. The pills Margaret gave me.

"Yes."

He nods and without another word, punches inside. I yelp, then suck in air, trying to work through the intrusion. It burns, the stretching of my inner walls, but pain isn't my enemy. Pain is something I crave to endure. His father taught me that with the hours of relentless lessons, the years of sacrifice, the intensity of Correction. Pain is something I understand, and I emit a whimper, wanting more.

A frown tugs at his mouth and rocks his hips into me. "Does it hurt?" he asks, not stopping.

"Do you want it to?" I ask, because I'm here to please him.

He expression shutters, and he grabs my inner thigh, pushing it wide. The sensation is different, deeper, and a moan builds in my chest. Silas showed me enough about my body to know what it likes. Levi taught me though Corrections what I crave. And Elon... under his darkness, I felt the true heat of passion—I understand *want*. I'm too scared of Rex to feel any of these things, too intimidated by his perfect body, by his cold stare, by the power he holds inside this bed and out. By his birthright.

I lay rigid while he thrusts into me, mute as he rocks his hips with rugged force.

"Jesus," he mutters, followed by a string of swear words. "It's nice that you're tight, but fuck, you need to let me in."

I don't know what that means, how to be what he wants.

"Unclench a little," he commands, pulling out before slamming back in.

He tears through me, a different sort of innocence stripped away. I smell his body, his scent. I feel the slick heat of his sweat as our bodies slap together. I close my eyes, floating away as he grows more erratic, the grunts coming faster, his hips pummeling into me.

My whole body is tense when he comes and I peek at him, at his clenched jaw, spine stiff, his manhood pulsing deep inside, filling me with his seed. I feel no more lonely when he pulls out than I did when he was inside of me, although when I move to close my legs, he holds them apart, one finger scooping up his seed and pushing it back inside.

I'm still lying there, sticky cum between my legs, pulse pounding from the lack of my own release, confused and conflicted. This is all I'd ever wanted. All I'd ever dreamed.

After all the trials and tribulations, that one act seals it.

Rex and I are officially Bonded Mates.

2

———

S ilas

THE BEDROOM DOOR OPENS, and I look past Rex's frame to catch a glimpse at Imogene. All I see is a her naked on the bed before the door snaps shut.

My friend passes, and I reach for the knob.

"Don't you dare go in there."

"And why the fuck not?"

Rex sighs, running his hand through his hair. "Because you'll go in there and hover over her like some mama hen. She needs a minute, and I need to talk to you."

Rex is my best friend—one of them at least—but at all times he outranks us and although I've defied him before, I know now is not the time.

Elon and Levi are both in the living room. Elon sits in an armchair, his body almost too big for the space. His eyes search

Rex's as he walks in the room. "You ready to tell us what the fuck is going on?"

"I changed my mind," he says, walking to the refrigerator. He skips the door, moving to the cabinet above where he unearths a bottle of whisky—contraband, but who is going to tell him no? He unscrews the top and takes a long swig. His shirt is untucked. His pants are wrinkled. His face has the pink flush of a man who'd just exerted himself. "We're Bonded. In the eyes of my father, there's no going back."

The last we knew Rex was leaving Serendee. He'd been threatening it for years and after his father's birthday weekend things reached a climax. None of us expected him to show up for the ceremony—or to claim Imogene as his mate.

"So you stayed," Levi says. "Why?"

He looks to me. I'd shown him exactly what happened to women that were not tied to a man in Serendee—women that held Anex's interest. "Does there have to be a reason?" Rex asks. Elon snorts. Even Levi rolls his eyes. He leans against the doorframe. "What?"

"You do nothing without a reason," Elon says. "It's either self-serving or to get back at your father."

"Maybe this time it's both."

It probably is.

"So what?" Levi asks. "You brought her back here immediately following the ceremony and staked your claim?"

"You don't get to tell me how to run my Bonding, Levi." Rex narrows his eyes. "She's mine. Not yours."

"You say that," Elon starts, "but you leave her to us to mold into the woman you want. Were you not happy with the way Levi put meat on her bones? Or the sexy lingerie I bought her before you tore them off? Or the fact Silas tended to her after you ripped her virginity from her so ruthlessly?"

"In the eyes of my father and all of Serendee, she is mine and mine alone," Rex says, crossing his legs at the ankle, "but you're right, this is less about me and more about exposing my son of a bitch father for being a fraud and a predator. I'm also not inclined to give him what he wants, which," his eyes dart to mine, "Silas pointed out to me before the ceremony, is Imogene."

Levi's eyes widen with alarm. "You want to expose him for what? Rex, I know you and Anex have years of problems. I know you think—well," Levi can't say it, '*You think your father killed your mother,*' but we all know it. "Does she know this is your plan?"

"Not that it's any of your business," Rex says, "but I made my demands clear to Imogene before we stepped into the ceremony. We made an agreement."

"What kind of agreement?" Levi asks. His devoutness to Serendee is being put to the test, and sometimes I wonder if he'll eventually break under Rex's Lapses.

"She's to be available to me and to meet my needs at all times. And in return I will play the part of her Mate in front of my father and the other residents of Serendee while I continue to collect evidence of his manipulations."

"What do you mean by play the part?" I ask. Everything about this made me uneasy. It was one thing when it was the four of us humoring Rex's ideas but dragging in an innocent like Imogene made me anxious.

"I've agreed to come home at night. Every night."

Elon's eyebrow raises. "You're abstaining from other women?"

He hesitates, which isn't a surprise. Rex has never denied himself of anything especially the excess found in the secular world. "She's right to want me to come home at night but... she's not ready to meet my needs." He pushes off the wall, eyes meeting each of ours. "She's too timid and unsure. She's still too fucking compliant." I think of her small frame and shiny blonde hair. "I want you to continue with her training."

"You're sure about that?" Elon asks. They're both still sporting the bruises from fighting over her. "You can handle the three of us being with her?"

"Yes. I'm asking you to do it this time—not Anex. That's the difference."

"I'm in," I say, unwilling to give up a chance to be close to her. To protect her from Anex's plans. "Whatever you need."

Rex looks at Elon. He nods. The hold out, of course, will be Levi. He may not be devoted to Anex, but he believes deeply in the tenants of Serendee. It's the foundation of his entire persona. Without it, I don't know who or what Levi would be.

Even so, it's not a surprise when he says, "I'll continue to offer my guidance," because I've seen the effect Imogene has had on him; body, mind, and soul. He wants her as much as the rest of us.

What isn't said aloud is that although Rex claims her as his own, Imogene is not the kind of woman that can be bound to one man. She belongs to all of us.

3

I mogene

THE MESSAGE COMES the next morning, before I leave for work. I have an appointment at the healer. Even though the office is located downstairs, I still need an escort through the maze of hallways that crisscross their way through the main house.

"Is something wrong?" I ask before Healer Bloom can even speak. The last time I saw her was the day of The Ordering, when she did a physical to confirm my innocence.

"No," she replies, giving me a tight smile. "Standard procedure after the Bonding Ceremony."

I frown. "But it was just yesterday, that seems very fast."

"Not if your Mate is Anex's son."

"Oh," I say, flattening my hand over my stomach. "His father wants to know if we've consummated the Bonding."

"With their strained relationship, everything is over scrutinized."

"We have," I tell her, feeling the heat in my cheeks. "Bonded."

"I'm sure that is true, but an examination is mandatory." Just like last time she waits while I undress, taking forever to unbutton my dress. I feel her eyes on me as she assesses the non-approved undergarments. I'm to wear secular bras and panties for Rex. She whips out her measuring tape. "You've gained weight."

"At the request of my mate," I explain, knowing that with anyone other than Rex that would be a sign of disobedience. "He prefers a woman with more flesh."

She hums her disapproval. "I suppose he likes the lace under-garments as well."

He does, although Elon picked them out, and I've seen the way Silas has reacted to them. I'd venture to guess all men like them. I swallow. "Yes."

She catalogues my body, running her finger over a pale mark on my wrist. "These marks?"

"From Correction. Everything is documented in my logs." I don't tell her that I no longer give self-correction. Levi has taken over that duty.

Another hum, this one less negative. "Get on the table."

I lay back and once again the bright light shines in my face, making me unable to see anything else in the room. I hear Healer Bloom shuffling about, the roll of her instrument cart, the soft snick of a drawer opening and shutting. She directs me to place my feet in the stirrups, tapping the insides of my knees. "Spread apart, Imogene."

The room grows quiet under her examination, but this time something is different. I understand the touch of a man now. I know the parts of my body that provide pleasure and sometimes pain. The hot button of my clitoris and the deep canal of my vagina. As Healer Bloom examines my body, fingers brush against my clit sending a shuddering wave up my body. I jolt up, moving to shade my eyes from the light, but two hands pin me down by the shoulders.

"What—"

"Shhh, Imogene, settle down." Warm fingers stroke my inner thigh.

Bile rises in the back of my throat. There's no mistaking the voice. Anex.

"What are you doing?" I ask, pulling against the hands holding me down, but they are strong and powerful.

"It's my duty to make sure my son is following through with his commitment to you." I feel the pressure of a finger at my entrance, pushing at the barrier. "You know the problems that I've had with him, the sacrifices I've made to keep him part of Serendee." One finger pushes in, then a second. "It would be just like him to pretend he Bonded with you."

"Why would he do that?"

He chuckles. "To manipulate. Play mind games. To keep you from me." He curls his fingers and my body clenches, trying to expel the invasion. "If he hadn't stepped up at the Ceremony, Imogene, you would have become mine by default. You would have been Fallen and come under my care and training." He feels around for a moment longer and sighs. "It seems as though he staked his claim, didn't he?" He shifts and whispers close to my ear, "Was he gentle when he took you? Or did he barrel into you with the finesse of a bull on a rampage?"

I gasp at his crassness, but he just slips his fingers out of my body as quickly as they intruded. I feel hollow. Repulsed. The light swings away, and all I see are white spots. Blinking them away, I see him standing over the table, handsome. Powerful. Terrifying.

"I want you to understand that I'm watching you." He sniffs his fingers, inhaling my scent, before cleaning them with a cloth. "All of you, and if there's any sign that this relationship is a farce or worse, an attempt to usurp my position, all of you will suffer. Do you understand?"

I nod, wrapping an arm around my stomach, willing the contents of my breakfast to stay down. He isn't just threatening me and Rex. He's threatening the guys as well. "Yes. I understand."

"Good." He offers his hand and obediently, I take it. He leans forward, speaking right in my ear. "Now that he's tasted your tight little pussy, don't expect my son to remain interested. It's a novelty that he'll grow restless of soon."

"Rex and I are Bonded, Anex. In front of you and all of Serendee. I have faith that I can be a good mate and that he won't grow restless of me."

"I hope you're right." He steps back and lifts his hand, ghosting it over my hair. "But if you're wrong, don't worry. I'll always have a room reserved for you." His grin is dark. Wicked. "It's right next to the one I saved for your mother."

As I RUSH to the recruitment office for my shift, I'm forced to reconcile that Rex's indifferent Bonding the night before was more than him just getting off. He was protecting me from his father.

I wasn't a virgin—he'd taken that from me before the ceremony. And I'd had sex with Silas later. But Anex has made it clear he knows everything going on in Serendee. In our private quarters and in our beds. We can't be too careful. Our leader seems too eager for his son to fail.

I'm caught between two powerful men and it's my duty to try to keep the peace.

I manage to work the rest of the day, filing interest forms for potential recruits and organizing pamphlets for members to pass out on the college campus nearby. The upscale University allows a fertile recruiting ground, with so many young people seeking Enlightenment. I always believed I was doing good work by sitting at this desk; that I'd been chosen by Anex because of my character and proof of responsibility. Now, the twisting uneasiness in my stomach is a reality check. Anex has kept an eye on me because of my mother's betrayal—and has been looking for any opportunity to announce a claim on me for his own purposes.

I'm cleaning up my desk when the door opens. I sense his presence before I see him—broad and imposing. Rex appears before me, features tense.

"Rex," I say, smoothing down the front of my dress. His eyes sweep over me, and I wonder if he can tell that I'd been examined —that his father's fingers had been inside of me. "Are you teaching today?"

"No. I was just finishing up on campus and thought I'd stop by to see you home."

"Oh." I'm shocked, but we'd agreed to behave like a Bonded couple. I suppose that's what this looks like. "That would be wonderful. Let me get my things."

I hurry, not wanting to annoy him. His temper is sharp, less explosive, and more honed than the blade of a knife. He opens the door for me, allowing me to go first and when we step onto Main Street, he takes the position next to the sidewalk, protecting me from the passing traffic.

"So you worked on campus today?" I broach, hoping I don't sound lost and clueless. I am. Outside of stealing a cake from his father's birthday celebration and a disastrous picnic, we've barely had a normal conversation.

"I had a few deliveries," he says, eyes watchful as we pass a series of restaurants with seating on the sidewalk. I don't miss the judgment from the patrons as they take in my hand sewn dress. I'm accustomed to the looks, but what's unusual is the way the women's eyes slide right over me and straight to Rex. It's well known in our community how handsome he is, but clearly secular women really do find him as attractive. He seems completely unaware of that as he continues, "Then, I set up another transaction for one of the fraternity houses."

"Selling the product under the barn?" I ask quietly.

He frowns. "Elon shouldn't have shown you that."

"You're right," I say. "You should have been the one to tell me the truth about the businesses Serendee operates under our noses."

The muscle in the back of his jaw tenses and he grabs me by the bicep, pulling me away from a line of people waiting to be seated.

He doesn't let go once we're past them, instead pushing me down the alley that leads to the entrance of our community. My breath is knocked out of me as he tosses me hard against the wall. "He shouldn't have told you because it's dangerous. It's not a place for a woman like you."

"Like me?" I ask. "What does that mean?" Does he think I'm untrustworthy, like my mother? A betrayer of Serendee?

His hand is flat against the wall next to my head and our eyes level. "An innocent. A follower of The Way. Someone that doesn't need the burden of Serendee's true weight on her shoulders."

"You don't trust me."

His eyes narrow. "Other than the feel of your pussy clenching around my cock when I'm inside of you, I don't know you, Imogene."

My jaw drops, the shock of his crassness overtaking any other emotion. It's not the first time he's treated me like this. He's a disgusting pig. He's assaulted me more than once. And here I am, Bound to him. God, I'm a fool.

Maybe I should have just let Anex have what he wants.

A hot tear burns at the corner of my eye. Humiliation—and not the first I've experienced today. "I'm no longer an innocent," I say, "You and your father took that option away from me the day you arranged to make me your mate. And the moment I accepted the Order, the weight of this community fell to my shoulders, because you and I are one. We are Bonded. In the eyes of Serendee, and it was sealed when you pushed past my barrier and left your seed inside of me." I place my hands on his hard, muscular chest. "If you don't think you know me, then figure out a way to find out, because I have no choice but to stand by your side."

His eyes narrow. "You spoke to him. Anex. When? Today?"

My cheeks burn. "Healer Bloom examined me." I can't bring myself to say that Anex had done the actual exam. "She gathered proof that we're truly Bonded. Your father," I swallow, "he was there."

His hand clenches around my arm. "Did he touch you?" Before I can answer he tightens his grip and repeats, "Did he?"

I see the dark, murderous, glint in his eye, and I understand then that Rex is hanging by a thread. He's looking for an excuse and he'll end his father if given the chance. I can't allow that. What if he fails? What happens to me then? What happens to Elon, Silas, and Levi without the protection of their best friend?

"No," I tell him, wincing at the pain of his fingers digging into my skin. "No. He was just there for confirmation, but he's watching us. Closely."

He registers my pain and releases me. My arm throbs, but I take the chance to duck under his arm and hastily walk toward the gate. I fumble with the latch, and his hand comes down over mine, taking over. He stops me before I walk through.

"If he approaches you again, let me or Elon know."

"I will."

"I won't allow him to hurt you, Imogene."

"Why not?" I ask, pushing past him, exiting the secular world for the safety of Serendee, "Or is hurting me something reserved just for you and your friends?"

WE WALK IN SILENCE, the hostility growing between us like bricks in a wall. I regret telling him he has to come home every night. All it will do is create pain. My pain. I'd be better off if he was off in the city, getting his needs met by secular women.

Except that thought makes my stomach hurt.

At the fork in the road, he stops. The main house, where we'd both been living, although separately, looms up the hill.

"We won't be going back to my father's house." He looks down the other road. "We'll live in a cottage like all of the other couples that went through the ceremony yesterday."

"Why?" Mixed emotions swirl in my stomach. In the Main

House there were always people around. Staff, guards, Anex's spiritual wives... but a cottage? That feels isolated.

"Because I need some space from him." He glances up at the imposing Main House. "He's a murderer. A criminal." His hand balls in a fist. "I can't be near him any longer, and I don't trust him with you."

His words should be comforting, but they just bring up conflict and turmoil. I've lived my whole life with Anex as my spiritual guide. I can admit things are confusing right now. Anex's behavior... it's discomforting, but he's told us many times that following him, and The Way, is not an easy path. Our own resistances will try to sway us. Our Regressive thoughts will creep in, trying to lure us away from the life he's built for us. I'm not ready to give that up because Rex is delusional and hurt because he lost his mother at a young age.

Join the club.

I follow him down the road, until he stops in front of a pale green house. I raise an eyebrow. "You think this is a cottage?"

He looks down at me, blue eyes cold as ice. "Compared to the mansion? Yes."

The house is a large, two-story, bungalow with a wrap-around porch. "It's quite big for the two of us."

He brushes his blonde hair out of his eyes. "Four bedrooms. One for us and one for each of the guys."

The big news here should be that he's suggesting we'll share a room and I assume a bed, but that's not what forces me to snap my eyes away from the house, toward him. "The guys?"

Elon, Levi, and Silas.

"They'll be living with us. Keeping an eye on you while I'm at work." 'Work' for Rex, means selling the drugs grown in secret underneath Serendee. The real funds Anex uses to bankroll his mission. It's the excuse Rex has to spend his time outside of Serendee around the gluttony of the secular world. He rests his hand on the porch railing and sweeps his eyes over me. "You'll continue with your job during the day at The Center, assuaging my father's suspicions, while I search for the truth about what really happened to my mother."

"And at night?" I ask, needing to be prepared for another round. "What are your expectations of me at night?"

His eyes sweep over me, and he steps close, tilting my chin up with a surprisingly gentle touch. "I expect you in my bed, ready for me."

My body trembles, remembering the ways he forcefully took me, claiming me hard and quick. The memory of pain flickers deep in my belly. Pain is something I've gotten used to, but not the shame that comes with it.

"Of course," I say, pushing the words past the lump in my throat. "Whatever you wish."

He holds my eye for a long moment, like maybe he wants to say more, but ultimately, he drops his hand and climbs the porch steps. There is no ceremony here. No happy couple crossing the threshold, no cake or champagne waiting on the kitchen table or homemade goods from members of the community.

It's just the two of us, both treading water, trying to cling to something that makes sense.

Unfortunately, in this scenario, neither of us can swim and in the end, we'll both drown under the weight of one another.

4

E lon

ALL OF MY belongings are already at the cottage when I arrive. They've been brought over, I assume, by some of the workers in the Main House. There's a whole hierarchy in Serendee. At the top are the Chosen, the inner circle. At the bottom... well, visibly they are people wanting Anex's favor. The minions that do the grunt work around the community. Less visibly? That would be the Fallen, or those who have gone against Anex and The Way. They are not even worthy of carrying my boxes from one house to the other. Their time is spent isolated and in penance.

I've never felt out of step with my place in Serendee. My friendship with Rex solidified my position years ago, but something shifted in the last twenty-four hours. Rex did the right thing by standing by Imogene, but I'm not sure that's what his father really wanted or how the fallout will affect all of us.

"Is anyone here?" I call out, walking down the hall. The

bedrooms are on the second floor. Levi and Silas' are both empty, their beds stacked with moving boxes. The master bedroom door is closed, but the faint glow of light shines underneath the gap.

I knock and hear Imogene's soft voice from the other side. "Come in."

When I open the door, I'm not prepared for the sight of her. Not sitting in bed, wearing a little black negligee, made of more lace than silk. It's one of the ones that I bought for her and with the extra meat on her bones she has cleavage that wasn't there a month ago. Her eyes widen when she sees me, and she tugs at the blanket to cover her body. I start to shoot her a command, to tell her to put her hands down and let me see her like this, but I remember things have changed. She's now a Bonded female. Rex says he wants us to continue training her, but can I really still force her to my will?

"I thought you were Rex." The red burn of her cheeks travels down her neck to her chest, making it hard not to look. "He's not here, if you're looking for him. He brought me here, showed me the room and told me he was going out for a while."

Only Rex would leave a beautiful woman waiting half-naked in his bed out of some possibly misguided defiance to his father.

Despite his absence, he is still Imogene's betrothed. I shouldn't be standing here. I take a step back toward the hallway and she blurts, "He agreed to come home every night." I hesitate and raise an eyebrow. "That was the deal between us. He comes home every night and I..." she tries to pull the blanket up higher, "well, I have to do as he says. *Everything* he says."

I'm aware Rex took Imogene's virginity out on that dock in the lake. He and I got into a fight about it—a physical fight that left him with a black eye and me with a bruised fist. He felt like it was his right to claim her, but there are ways to do things in Serendee. Taking her like that, no matter how tempting it was, shouldn't have happened. He could have ruined her in the eyes of the community, or worse, the eyes of his father.

"If you're lucky," I say, thinking it's what she wants to hear, "he'll come home drunk and satisfied and leave you alone."

"You think he's with another woman?"

Oh *fuck*. Not what she wants to hear. Dammit. This is new to me, too.

I think a bit harder on how to respond to this. "I think he's spent a lifetime running away from his responsibilities and trying to dull the pain. Those habits are hard to break."

"Do you think his father killed his mother?"

I blink. I guess he told her his suspicions? That comes as a surprise. "I know Rex thinks that his father killed his mother. Are his suspicions real or delusions? I'm not sure." I walk back into the room and sit on the edge of the bed. "I know losing her almost broke him. Then later when he found the papers she left him, we were already starting to learn about the side of Serendee Anex keeps hidden from the rest of the community. He's struggled with his faith in The Way for a long time. That's why he runs wild when he's outside the walls."

"That kind of talk would get the rest of us tossed out of Serendee."

"Like your mother." Imogene's mother was a full-blown Regressive and had been banished when she was young. It's part of the reason Rex agreed to be Ordered to her. She knows what it's like to lose a mother and, no matter how hard she tries to be devout, defiance runs in her blood. "You won't get tossed out, Little Lamb." I take her hand, which causes the blanket to drop. I push my finger under the leather straps of her bracelet, feeling her warm skin. Rex wears a matching one, signaling their commitment. I stare at her mouth, remembering the kiss we shared when I showed her the secrets beneath the barn. "Rex claiming you made you legitimate. Chosen. Your loyalty won't be tested."

She bites down on her bottom lip and my eyes drop to the smooth skin between her breasts. She's not mine, I remind myself. No matter what liberties I took before. That had been commanded by Anex. I did my job. I made her ready. Bought her these lacy things—taught her how to wear them. Now she belongs to my best friend and is here for his needs, even if he's offered to share.

It's not what I really want. I want *her*, not scraps tossed to me by a friend.

"Somehow I doubt that," she says, quietly.

She may not be tested, but I know I will be. Just the sight of her cloaked in silk and lace... it would be so easy to push her against the pillows and take her right here. She wouldn't fight me. I know that from the pink in her cheeks and the way her chest rises and falls. If she did? There's part of me that knows why Rex did it—why he took her like that. Feeling this Little Lamb tremble beneath him?

It's tempting. Everything about her is tempting.

I look away and catch a glimpse of the two of us in the mirror. My dark hair hangs messily across my forehead and my eyes look wild. I'm exhausted from the weekend of celebration, of fighting, but none of that is what propels me to my feet. It's the way Imogene looks in the reflection—small and innocent. Sweet but sexy. Truly an innocent, vulnerable, little lamb.

And there's no doubt as I walk out of the room without another word, that I'm the big bad wolf.

It's not hard to find him. Like all other pack animals, he has a preferred hunting ground, and that's right where I find him. There are two rows of commercial business that surround the University. The Center took up one of these spots for our recruitment office, but otherwise, The Strip, as the college kids call it, is filled with restaurants, bars and other places to hang out. That's the first place Rex goes when he's looking for a quick hookup—and to fulfill his recruitment quota. Two birds, one stone—and hopefully an orgasm or two.

He's leaning against the brick wall just outside the bar towering over a cute redhead he's been putting the hardsell on for weeks now. Anex may be a conniving bastard but he knows how to sell his way of life—Serendee and The Way. Some people are already on a journey and seeking Enlightenment and walk in off the street. But a lot of these people need coaxing—and what better salesman than a guy who looks, and acts, like Rex.

The apple didn't fall far from the tree.

From the way his body is angled, his forearm resting on the wall, glass of alcohol in his fingertips, to the slight lean into the girl, the way he pushes a strand of hair off her shoulder, it's clear he's going in for the kill. Which is exactly why I need to stop him.

"Hey," I call, hands shoved in the pockets of my jacket. "Rex."

He looks up, eyes curious, but quickly shifting to annoyance. "Hey man."

"You need to come home."

He grins—it's for the girl. Cocky and sure. "I'm a little busy."

She glances over at me and does a double take. I don't have that golden boy thing going on like Rex, but I know I'm a good-looking guy. Built. Women are drawn to me.

"I'm sure," I reply. "But I need you back at the house."

His hand slides down her hip. "I'm sure you can handle it," he grins at the girl, "Katelyn and I were just going to go over some of the level one tenants, to see if she's interested in finding out more."

"Tenants, sure." I roll my eyes. I walk over and insert myself between the two of them. "Katelyn," I say, addressing her directly, "I hate to interfere, but do you think you can swing by the Center tomorrow? I'm sure someone, maybe even Rex, will be happy to discuss this further."

"Um..." she looks between us, eyes wide and confused. "I guess so."

"Thanks, sweetheart," I say, giving her my own persuasive grin. "I promise, whatever, um, *information*, my brother was about to give you, will be readily available at the Center during business hours."

Katelyn giggles, but walks off, engulfed by the group of students standing near the front of the bar. Once she's gone, Rex gives me the stink eye and says, "Seriously? What the fuck dude?"

"Your mate is waiting for you at home."

He scoffs. "Trust me, brother, she's better off with me here than at home." He looks wistfully toward the bar. "You realize I wasn't really going over Serendee info, right? I was about to get my dick sucked."

"Yeah, I'm aware, but unfortunately you're not a single guy anymore. You have obligations. At home."

His eyes narrow. "So, you're worried about the Little Lamb all the sudden? Really?"

"I am when I find her stressed and worried, waiting for you to come home."

"What the hell does she have to be stressed about?"

See that's the thing about Rex—or being Rex. He can just exist in his own reality. Sure, he has obligation to Serendee and Anex like the rest of us, but he has a long rope. No one has ever depended on him. "She's a fucking basket case. Totally unsure about her position, here. With you, with her dad, with her mother's history. She has no idea where she stands, which in my opinion, is exactly how your father wants it. I don't blame her for being nervous about it, because it feels like she's nothing but a pawn in a game being played by you and your father."

"If you're so worried about her, why don't you fuck her? I gave you permission."

Jesus. He'll never get it. Never. "You're a prick, you know that?"

"And you're overly invested in my life."

I laugh. God, this is rich. "You think I have a choice about that? You think I don't want to have my own life? My own options." I lunge forward, gripping the front of his shirt in my fist. "My own fucking mate?" I tilt my head, locking eyes. "That's not how our world works. So yeah, I did what I always do, what we all always do, follow up on the mess you leave behind." I nod to where Katelyn had just been pressed against the wall. "Who do you think is going to clean her up tomorrow? Smooth that over?"

Silas. We both know that. He'll be the one to meet her if she shows up tomorrow at the Center or track her down if she doesn't. He'll follow up, soothe her bruised ego and work his magic.

"Jesus, Elon. I'm just blowing off a little steam," he says, having the good sense to look a little guilty. I release him and he shakes his head. "Fucking Imogene... it's like screwing a plank. She just lies there, looking like she's waiting for it to be over."

I stare at him. "Then maybe you need to up your goddamn game."

He waves me off. "Nah. She's too much work."

Of course. That's why he's offered her to us. I get her dressed for him. Silas breaks her in. Levi works on her flaws. It's too late to argue about this—how could I? I'd be dealing with years of ingrained entitlement. I don't have that time—and honestly, it's not my place.

"Come on," I say, "I don't care what you do with her when you get home—just *go* home. You promised."

He relents, but not before finishing his drink. It's then that I notice how wasted he is and it's probably a good thing I showed up when I did. Rex may be Teflon inside Serendee, but outside? Things are different. People are watching and one false move could be a problem for everyone.

5

———

I mogene

THE SMELL INFILTRATES my dreams at the same time the bed shifts underneath me, jarring me from sleep. Before I can react a heavy hand weighs on my hip, then pins me by the arms. I blink, looking up at the figure in the dark. I can smell him; the spicy scent of alcohol on his breath, the leather from the bracelet I tied to his wrist. Rex straddles me, thighs on each side of my body, my arms caught in his grip.

"You're here," Rex says, running his hand over the side of my breast, "just like I told you to be, just like a good Little Lamb."

"You're drunk." My voice is raspy from sleep. I squirm but he clamps his thighs tighter, holding me in.

He laughs. "And a little high." His fingers reach between us, bunching up the silk and fingers the lace waistband of my panties. I stiffen and he says, "Calm down. I'm not going to hurt you."

The hard press of his erection against my lower belly says otherwise. At least he was true to this word and came home.

My mouth dries as I watch him lift slightly freeing himself from the confines of his pants. He's long and engorged, tip slippery already. The twist of fear and want wars in my blood. Pulse racing, heat building. Silas showed me it didn't have to hurt, but there's also something dark in me that knows I like pain. I think he likes it that way, too, and I brace myself.

He moves up my body, planting my arms under his knees, freeing his hands. He makes quick work of the silk top, tossing it on the floor. His hands move to my breasts, kneading them roughly. I swallow back a cry, knowing it will only encourage him.

"Remind me to thank Levi," he says, fingers circling my nipple and sharply tugging the peak.

"What?" Does he know about the Corrections? How pain turns to pleasure? "Why?"

"I know he encourages you eat more," he pushes my breasts together, enhancing the valley between them. "The results are worth it. Your tits are definitely bigger."

He bends, licking a hot trail between my breasts and then lathing his tongue over my nipple. I shiver from the feel of it, back arching. Rex laughs, his warm breath coating the wet skin. And he moves again, settling higher, pushing the tip of his cock between my breasts.

"What are you doing?"

"There's more than one way to fuck, you know that, Little Lamb?" His hands gather my flesh, and he slides his erection into the tight space. "It's not just the pussy, or even the mouth. Now that they're big enough, I can fuck your tits."

He thrusts into me again, sticky fluid coating the way. His hands hurt and his I fight for air. He bends over and whispers in my ear. "Just wait until I spread your cheeks and fuck you in the ass."

His words elicit the rush of warmth between my legs, I squirm beneath him. It seems to excite him, too, and he finds a rhythm, pushing and pulling his cock between my breasts. He's so dirty, so terribly bad, and this is not what I expect from my Mate. It's certainly not what I expect from the heir of Serendee.

His breath grows ragged, and I look up at his face; jaw clenched and tilted back. He's beautiful like this, with red cheeks and a slick sheen of sweat. His hair is pale, always catching light and giving off the hint of a halo. He's no angel. He's anything but. I should loathe him, but I've learned that my body and mind are not always in synch. Or maybe they are, and I just don't know what to do about it.

But that's why he picked me. I'm bad, too.

The soft flesh of my breasts feels numb from his rough handling and abuse, but I still feel it when he makes his final, lurching, groan, pinching his fingers deep into the skin. I cry out and close my eyes, feeling thick seed spill across my chest.

I lay under him like that, soiled and used, aware when he shifts back, releasing me from his weight. Without moving, I wait for the sound of him leaving, the gathering of his things and the slow exit. Instead, I sense the rustling of sheets and a soft cloth wiping off my chest. I open my eyes just in time to see him toss the cloth on the floor and kick off his pants. A moment later he's lying next to me. He's staying? He did say this was *our* bedroom. I curl up and away, facing the wall, pretending my heart isn't still pounding and that there's not a dull ache between my legs.

I shift my eyes away and stare at the wall next to the bed. There's a spider building a web in the corner of the windowsill, an insect trapped in the sticky threads. I watch its tiny legs spinning, faster and faster, as it approaches its prey. Rex curls behind me, his chest still rising and falling.

"Who told you to wear that outfit? My father?"

God. Gross. "No."

"Silas?"

Maybe he'll go away if I answer. "Elon."

"Did he now?" I don't have to see him to know the expression on his face. That his lips curve into a mix of cruel and amused. His arm slides around my waist, pulling me against his body. I don't trust the intimacy. I don't trust him.

"Yes. He took me shopping and brought me clothes that he thought you would like."

His fingers tug at the lace of my panties, thumb dipping underneath. I suck in a breath of air. "I bet he liked them, too. Did he touch you?"

I swallow and stare at the spider.

"He did, didn't he? You know, we've always liked the same things. The same cars, the same guns, the same women." He inches down between my legs, brushing against my clit. My reaction is a deep shudder and he chuckles in my ear. "Did he touch you here?"

"No."

His movement is so different from before, it's gentle and seductive. "You're so wet," he says, fingers slipping against my nerves. "I bet Silas gave you your first orgasm." He withdraws his hand, teasing. "Am I right?"

My hips rock forward, seeking friction. "Yes."

"He made it good for you, didn't he?"

He pushes a finger inside, curving it against the side. I sink into the feel of it, and he withdraws again. His voice hot against my ear. "Tell me what my brothers did to you, Little Lamb."

The demand is clear. Tell him and he'll get me off. I shouldn't want it, but the flame has been stoked. "Silas showed me TV shows. Movies. Elon kissed me and handled me a little rough, that's all."

He plunges his fingers into me again, applying pressure against my walls. His thumb holds against my clit, and I curl against him. Again, he withdraws. This time I cry out in frustration.

"And Levi?"

Do I tell him how Levi Corrects me? How he stole my panties after telling me to take them off and he spanked me until my flesh blistered? Levi told me Rex wouldn't like the levels of this kind of Correction. It's the kind of dedication to Serendee and The Way that he doesn't approve of.

His fingers hover over my entrance, slight pressure but not enough. He's mean enough that I know he'll walk out of here if I don't give him what he wants, and I'm desperate enough that I don't want him to. Still, I swallow the truth. "Levi is devout. He would never cross those lines, even if your father asked." I keep my eye on the busy spider, its tiny legs furiously spinning the web. Anything not to focus on the throbbing want between my legs.

"Thank you," he says, scraping the edge of my ear with his teeth. His fingers enter me again, this time with deliberate intent. He works me inside and out, drawing the orgasm out of me, in slow, incremental, waves. I push my face into the pillow as it rolls over me, the shudders wracking through my limps, stars bursting behind my eyelids.

Even after he withdraws his fingers for the last time, and the only sound in the room is my pulse pounding in my ears, he doesn't move, body close to mine. I tell him what I think he wants to hear.

"I won't let any of them touch me again."

He pushes the hair off my neck. "I wouldn't go that far."

For the first time, I turn to look at him. "What does that mean?"

He shrugs. "I've shared everything with them since we were kids. My house, my family, my *toys*." He touches my chin. "Why would I stop now?"

"But—"

"You belong to them as much as you belong to me. They're the ones that broke you in, eased you into being ready for me. It's not fair for me to take you for myself." He shifts his leg, his penis resting casually against his thigh. "Not that I told them that. They wouldn't accept it. I told them to continue their training."

"What are you talking about?" I know Rex is prone to extreme thoughts. Paranoia and maybe delusions but this seems insane. "You want to *share* me, with your best friends?"

"Brothers' really," he mumbles. "My father will never give them a mate of their own. He's got them right where he wants them— dependent on him and him alone. He'll keep pimping Silas out, he'll fuck and twist Levi's mind until he's the ultimate disciple, and he'll continue to harden Elon until there's nothing left but an angry shell." He wraps his arm around my waist and cinches it tight, pulling me into him. "They like you, Little Lamb, and I think you like them or at least how they make you feel."

My body blazes with heat. I feel called out—*seen*. But not in a good way. What he's suggesting and the simple fact I consider it for the tiniest moment is shameful. Indulgent. It's very, very bad.

I try to turn and face him, to tell him that he's lost his mind or maybe it's just another trick—a trap, but he's already asleep, eyes shut, lips slightly parted. His arm tightens around me, trapping me against his warm heat. I sigh and give up, my eyes returning to the spider, the only witness to what Rex is proposing. I thought when he claimed me at the ceremony that maybe things would make more sense. Now, I realize that I never left the web. If anything, it just grows bigger, stickier, and the more I struggle, the harder it is to escape.

WHEN I WAKE up the second time, it's lights out and I'm alone.

I don't know when Rex left or if he'll even remember coming in here. What I do know is that everything that he said last night confused me even more. He wants to share me with his friends, not just so they'll train me, but because he knows his father won't give them mates of their own.

He was drunk and despite what he said, *more* than a little high. If anything, it was a test of loyalty, to see if I'll betray him like my mother betrayed Serendee. What man would willingly share his wife with three other men?

I climb out of bed and go to the closet, pulling out a dress for work, ignoring the swirl of emotions which just thinking about intensifies. I skip breakfast, feeling the need to withhold. Everything in my life has been consumed with Indulgence lately. Sex. Clothing. Food. I take a minute to reflect in my journal, horrified at how I let things slip lately. I can't let Rex derail my path to Enlightenment.

The Center is busy, thankfully, with a steady stream of new

students coming in for classes. It allows me to focus on something other than myself. I see Levi once or twice. He has back-to-back sessions, instructing new recruits—most from the University. We don't speak, but the last time I was with him, Silas was burying himself inside of me while Levi held me in his arms. My cheeks burn when I think of the way he came against my back, breath ragged and warm.

After his class leaves, I pass him in the hallway. "Can we talk?"

His jaw tenses. "I have another class coming in, and I need to prepare."

"Right. I just…" I look over my shoulder to make sure we're alone. "I would like to schedule some time with you. Privately."

His eyebrow raises. "For Correction?"

I nod.

"Is this about the other night? Things got out of hand. I never should have—"

"It's not that." I pause, recalling our night together with Silas in the tent. Levi held me while Silas showed me what making love was really all about, instead of the harsh brutality Rex had shown me. "Well, not specifically. It's just everything going on over the weekend, the Bonding ceremony, and our new living situation, I feel very off balance."

"I'm not sure we should continue meeting now that you are Bonded."

Panic flares in my chest. Sheer, unbridled anxiety. I reach out and grab him by the arm. "Levi, I need this. I need something normal in my life." His expression doesn't change. "Rex told me last night he's okay with me continuing my training with each of you."

"He's expressed the same to us, but," his forehead furrows, "I'm not sure that means he's okay with me being your Guide? You know how he feels about Anex's procedures."

"I know that Rex doesn't believe in The Way. Not like you do. I know that you and I are caught between two warring men. Father and Son." My words are a whisper—inappropriate to be said aloud.

Levi nods in understanding. "I've agreed to balance both and I need your Guidance to do that."

His hesitation is brief. As it should be. Rex may be his best friend, but he is loyal to our beliefs.

"Okay. We can schedule something," he looks at his watch, "but not today. Tomorrow?"

Relief rushes through me. "Yes, thank you."

His smile is tight. "You're welcome, Imogene."

I watch Levi walk away, thinking that if Rex thinks this man likes me he is very confused. I'm pretty sure I am nothing but an albatross around all of their necks. A naïve, little lamb that needs constant education and attention. I'm sure they have much better things to do with their time.

When I get back to my desk, an envelope is propped up against the phone with my name on it. The lobby is empty, but someone must have come in while I was in the back. I open it and see a typed invitation.

The time has come.
For you to embrace your Enlightenment.
If you're ready, wait by the oak tree at dusk.
Prepare for the future.

INSTANTLY, I know this is the invitation to the women's group Margaret, one of Anex's spiritual wives, told me about. A smile spreads across my face. I'd wondered, after so much uncertainty with Rex, if I would still be considered. But here it is. These women want me to be part of their group. Hell yes, I'm ready.

6

———————

S ilas

"You're late," Elon says, shifting over on the sofa to give me some room. His nose wrinkles. "Jesus, you smell like pussy."

I sniff my fingers. "It's vanilla." To be fair, the guys are used to the oily scents following my massage sessions with recruits. To them vanilla probably does smell like pussy. "And Kayla is demanding a lot of my time. I need Anex to decide what he wants to do about her."

Kayla is one of the recruits from outside of Serendee. She is the heir to a trillion-dollar company and seeking meaning in her life. Anex is willing to allow outsiders into Serendee for a price: loyalty, dedication, commitment, and cash. My job is to make them comfortable, to show them a taste of Enlightenment. His is to lock them, and their bank accounts, in for life.

"Do you know what this is about?" Levi asks, his knee bounces up and down. "Is Rex coming?"

"Rex is down in the barn prepping a batch for delivery," Elon says, "so whatever we're doing here, it's probably about him."

We'd been called to the little sitting room up in Anex's quarters. This isn't the first time we've been here. He often uses this room for instruction and personal meetings, but with everything going on with Rex and Imogene, I can't help but be a little apprehensive. I'd shown Rex the rooms where the Fallen are kept and told him that this is where Imogene would go if he rejected her. It seems more and more obvious that Anex's interest in her go far beyond being Rex's mate.

He wants her. I'm just not sure if it's to enact revenge on her mother's Regression, or if it's for something different. Either way, the desire to keep her safe is strong. I suspect the same from Elon and Levi.

The interior door opens and Anex walks in. He's alone, which is unusual, and makes me even more apprehensive. Elon is stiff as a rod next to me, and Levi's knee doesn't stop bouncing until we stand in unison, touching our foreheads and giving him a slight, respectful bow. We may be in the inner circle here, but everything we've done lately is uncharted territory. Like everyone else in Serendee, we're not immune to Correction

"Boys," Anex says, smiling warmly. "Thank you for coming to see me on such short notice."

Opting out of a meeting with Anex is unheard of. Most people in Serendee would love this opportunity of a private audience with our leader, but most people don't know what he's capable of. Who he is in private.

There's a soft knock on the door and a woman enters, carrying a tray of tea. She's young. She keeps her head down, not making eye contact with Anex. I catch a glimpse of her profile and recognize her. Her name is Bethany and she is being punished for kissing a boy before she came of age and received her Order. She's one of the Fallen, and this is the first time I've seen her out of the locked room.

Anex waits as she serves the tea, her hands shaking as she pours the steaming liquid into the china. The cuff of her sleeve draws up, and I can't help but notice the red welt circling her wrist. He watches her closely, observing her every move. When she's finished, he says, "You can go back to your room now, Bethany."

"Yes, sir," she replies, shuffling back out the door.

Anex shakes his head when she is gone and says, "That one has a dark streak of Regression inside of her. Born and raised here, but the darkness still crept inside. It's a problem, one that I'm creating a solution to, but in the meantime, I'm working with her—individually. I'm confident she'll progress." He takes a sip of tea and then smiles. "Now, I know you're not interested in the mundane aspects of my responsibilities and are wondering why I brought you up here today?"

Levi and I nod, while Elon mutters an affirmative.

"Now that Rex and Imogene are settled, I want to talk to you about a program Margaret has started. It's a women's group, a place for them to support and encourage one another as they follow The Way."

"A women's group?" Levi says. He teaches many of the men's classes down at the center. Viri Regum Sunt: Men Are Kings. "Like VRS."

"Similar," he says, "but obviously not the same. As you're aware, the needs of a woman are uniquely different from a man. They desire to belong. They need constant approval and have an absolute weakness for Indulgence." He lists these flaws with confidence and authority, adding, "While our masculine predisposition is to conquer and dominate. It's what sets us apart."

Elon frowns. "Why do you want to talk to us about a women's group. Isn't that... um, for women to handle?"

"You'd think," Anex says, "but no. Even in the biblical myths, Eve was created from Adam's rib. There is no Eve without Adam. No female without the male. Our ancestors knew this truth. Biology understands these facts. But like the participants in VRS, these women need to feel the support of other women, the confidentiality of their gender. As with everything else, we will provide the structure." He holds his teacup between his long, thin fingers.

"And you three, specifically, will see to Imogene's journey in the group."

"Imogene," Levi blurts. "She's joining?"

"She's been invited, and she's eager to get to know the other women, but as you know she's different. Like the Regressive that just left here," he glances toward the door, "there's a virus that burns under her skin. I can't let her infect the others."

"What do you want us to do?" I ask, feeling uneasy.

"I want her monitored every step of the way." He nods at Levi. "She'll come to you for Correction. She'll feel guilty for keeping secrets from Rex, for being different, for her sexual urges." He gives him a knowing look, and Levi's cheeks turn pink. "Continue to help her find Enlightenment and keep her in check."

"Y-yes. I can do that."

"Silas."

I jerk my chin up. "Yes?"

"There's going to come a time when you'll be needed to provide what only you can offer. Prepare her for that day and for the aftermath."

I have no idea what this means or what he wants from me, but I nod. What else is there for me to do? I've taught her how to pleasure herself and others. I've shown her love and compassion. I've healed her wounds.

"And me?" Elon asks.

"Your role is always the same, son," Anex gives him a stern look. "Protect Serendee and the leadership inside. These women will be required to provide collateral. I need you to collect and assess the threat of their confessions."

Elon and Anex hold one another's eyes for a long beat, and although my friend nods in agreement, assuring Anex that he will do what is needed of him, I get the distinct feeling these two are no longer on the same side. I'm not sure any of us are, things have shifted so dramatically lately, but to protect our lives—and Imogene's—we have no choice but to submit to our leader's commands.

"What about Rex?" Elon asks. "Does he know about this group?"

He leans back in his seat, expression grave. "In order for the females to fully immerse themselves in this movement, mates will not know that their partners are participating. The women will be told specifically to keep their involvement a secret. Rex can't know that it is anything beyond a standard support group. You three, outside of myself, are the only men aware that this group exists."

Another secret, like the one where he asked us to train Imogene for Rex. That didn't go over well. He'd lashed out at her and threatened to leave. We'd barely been able to keep him from going. I busy myself with my tea, not wanting to look at Anex or the others. There is no way this ends in anything other than hurt and betrayal.

Which, I think, may be exactly what Anex wants.

7

———

I mogene

THE OAK TREE stands by the edge of the forest, on a hill that allows for a magnificent view of Serendee. It's a significant marker in the community—the place where Anex realized the potential of the space. He stopped at this tree and declared the land the perfect spot to build his vision of utopia. My mother was there that day, notebook in hand, jotting down details for what would later become the blueprint for designing our self-sustaining home.

Now, as I approach the tree, I wonder what she would think about me being Bonded to Rex and joining this secret women's group—being a part of the Chosen. As much as I'd like to think she'd be happy for me, that I'd overcome the dark legacy she'd left me with, I know that isn't true. She would be horrified to know I'm tied to Anex—the man who was forced to banish her from her home and family.

There's a basket under the tree and a stack of white handker-chiefs. Attached is a note that says, "Cover your eyes and wait."

I look around, wondering if anyone is watching, but, other than the sound of nature, it's quiet. Carefully, I fold the bandanna and wrap it around my eyes, tying at the back of my head. I lean my backside against the tree and wait. I have no concept how long I wait, but eventually the snap of a stick alerts me that someone is nearby.

"Are you ready to start your journey?" the female voice asks.

"Yes." I'm both nervous and excited as I try to orient myself to her voice. A strong hand clasps around my wrist and leads me off the path. Even blindfolded, I can tell we've entered the forest. My skirt drags against the low growing shrubs, and my escort quietly guides me over roots and rough terrain.

"Can you tell me where we're going?" I ask once we're deep in the woods.

"You'll find out soon enough."

Sweat beads on my back by the time she slows, the hike leveling out and into a field. I smell the smoke before I hear movement—the shuffling and squish of soft dirt underfoot—and feel the warm heat and crackle of a fire. When the blindfold is removed, I blink, taking in the scene.

There are five others like me, all positioned around a large fire pit dug into the soft dirt. I recognize a few of them. Most are older than I am, their mates in the higher rungs of Anex's circle. Although, one woman catches my eye—she's someone Silas has recruited. Kayla is her name. I've seen her name in the files at The Center. Her family is wealthy, and she came here seeking something more than her family's power. I'm surprised to see a recruit here, but it's not my place to question, and I focus on the other women, the ones draped in green robes, their faces obscured by a large, draping hood.

"Welcome kindred souls, we're honored you've come to join us in our quest of empowerment," Margaret's voice rings out from the cluster of robed women. "What you're about to experience will tap into Anex's wise lesson and help you become a fuller, more Integrated being."

The sun drops behind the trees, dropping the temperature. One of the other robed women steps forward and commands us to undress.

Having grown up in the Domum, I'm accustomed to disrobing in front of other females. I quickly unfasten the buttons on my dress and allow it to drop over my narrow shoulders and waist. The only self-consciousness that I feel is from the weight gain over the last few weeks. Rex wants a woman with curvier hips and plumper breasts. I've been allotted more food than normal, but I hope the other women don't notice my Indulgence.

A cool breeze rustles in the trees, pushing past the heat of the fire.

"You're laid bare," Margaret says, "as a sign of rebirth. Coming into this group the same way you came into this world, naked, innocent, unbiased—but most of all vulnerable. Females do not like to be vulnerable, to show the weakness that lies in the essence of our being. This group is here to show you that embracing these traits makes you stronger."

She walks around the circle, assessing each of us as she goes. There's a firm kindness in her expression, a knowledge that I crave to possess. This isn't a woman that allows her insecurities to rule her life. She accepts who she is.

"Like a babe fresh from the womb, you will start at the bottom. Latched to the breast of another, wiser woman who will guide you through this journey. When you ascend again, you will not be the same person you are today. You're getting a second chance to grow into a fully Integrated female, attuned to The Way."

Her words inspire a surge of giddiness through me. Who doesn't want a chance to start over, to be absolved of your sins and embrace The Way? Through this emotion I try to absorb everything Margaret says: we will report to a "Main," who will guide us in our journey. She'll push us to our limits; exploring everything from pain to shocking self-awareness. Our renewal will be affirmed with a "birthmark," pressed into our skin as a symbol of starting new. We will be required to submit Collateral, because joining this group is an honor, a gift, and we must sacrifice something of our own in order to embrace what's being given. And at the end, when we are already to ascend into a fully formed, new being, The Way will test us, physically and emotionally, to confirm that we are worthy.

The leaders fan out, approaching each of us with a white robe. Margaret steps behind me, draping the robe over my shoulders.

"Put this on," Margaret says, in my ear but also loud enough for everyone to hear. "Feel the swaddling of the soft cotton, as if you're being wrapped for the first time." Her hands are gentle, but firm and I relax, truly feeling the gravity of the moment. "Thank Anex for allowing us this opportunity to be better."

As a group, we verbally thank our leader for his wisdom.

"One last thing," she says, going back to stand in front of the fire with the others. "This is a group for women, by women, you may not tell anyone outside of the group about what happens here. Not your Mate, not your family. This is a private journey that you must take alone. Your support comes from your Main." She holds up her hands. "Come, clasp hands and join me around the fire."

As the others rush forward, I find myself hesitating, feeling a twinge of doubt. Secrets don't go over well with Rex—especially when they come from the directive of his father's spiritual mate. It's also hard to keep anything from the others. Elon is naturally suspicious. Levi is well connected to the inner circle, and Silas has a way of getting me to share my private thoughts. Unlike the other women attending this ceremony, I have four men I must keep in the dark.

I think back to that day, so long ago, when Rex and I sat on top of the cliff as children. He'd hated me even then. I'd always been tainted in his eyes, and I always will be. Perhaps this cleansing, this rebirth, will be what I need to do to make him love and accept me as something other than a body to abuse, or a way to get back at his father.

I glance at the fire and then back at Margaret, the flames giving her hair a wild glow. Our eyes meet and her lips curve into an encouraging smile, her hand waving me to come closer, and the worries fade away.

8

———

I mogene

I WAKE up the next morning feeling giddy for the first time in... well maybe ever. *Renewed* is the word I'm looking for. I feel like a different woman, empowered and ready to take on the challenges of my household. If that's the power the women hoped to impart, I'm feeling it.

The sound of a low snore draws my attention to the other side of the bed. Rex is asleep. He must have come in after I did and for once didn't wake me to fill me with his seed. I prop up on my elbow, taking in the man next to me. He's on his side, facing the closet, shirtless, his skin a warm tan from his time in the sun. His hair is darker now, not the white blond from his childhood but still golden. His features sharp and appealing—the cut of his jaw darkened by stubble. He's got the body of a man—they all do—and it's one thing I find so jarring. I never experienced boys past the age of twelve. We were segregated and now that I'm confronted with it, even passively, everything about his physique seems different and strange.

I peer over him, eyes roaming over his hard abdomen. The trail of golden hair that vanishes under the white sheet. Emboldened by the gathering the night before, and my resolve to better things between me and my mate, I push the sheet down and rest a hand on his hip.

He shifts, not waking, but twisting toward me. My hand travels the slope of his hip until it's resting more on the hard muscle of his lower abdomen. My cheeks burn even though no one is looking at me. No one knows my Indulgent thoughts.

Carefully, I unpeel the sheet, revealing the darker thatch of hair and his cock resting against his thigh. What startles me is the fact it is already thick, hard from erection. Silas taught me about this, 'morning wood' is the slang for it. I get it.

I want to touch it.

Gathering my courage, I move my hand to his thigh, muscular and strong. I run my finger over the tip and instantly clear fluid builds. Rex shifts, but I'm focused on his body. The hard elegance— a body I know can be turned into a weapon in a blink. I remember how he's used it on me. In my mouth at the club that night, forcing me to swallow. On the dock when he took my innocence. The cold way he Bonded with me and the way he came on my tits.

I pull my hand back, reconsidering when—

"What are you doing, Little Lamb?" His voice is rough. Gritty from sleep.

I freeze and tilt my head. "I-I—" All that comes out is a stutter.

He reaches out, warm fingers tilting my chin upward. "Use your words. Why are you touching my dick?"

"I-I—" I swallow. "You looked so peaceful. Quiet. And you graciously let me sleep last night. I thought maybe I could show you my appreciation the way a mate would."

He shifts around, propping on his elbow so he's facing me. From this angle his erection looks impossibly larger. Or maybe it *is* larger. My heart pounds and a sense of inadequacy fills me. As though he knows, a small smile lingers on his mouth. "How exactly would you do that?"

"I could, uh, touch it?" The heat in my face quadruples. "Until you reach completion."

His eyebrows raise in a way that makes me feel foolish. "You want to give me an orgasm?"

"Yes. A handjob—that's what Silas called it right?" I'm so flustered, so out of my element that my palms start to sweat. "Unless you would rather me not."

His forehead creases at Silas' name, but a moment later it smooths back out. "Let me tell you one thing, Little Lamb, no man is ever going to decline an orgasm first thing in the morning." He stretches on his back, arms behind his head, elbows bent. Although he's the picture of calm, his cock rises between his legs, eager with anticipation. "Ready when you are."

I try to remember everything Silas taught me: *Act confident. Men love to have their cocks touched. Don't act nervous. Enjoy it. You're giving someone pleasure—that's a good thing, especially if he's someone you care about.*

Do I care about Rex? I ask myself, building up the nerve to take him in my hand. His lower belly dips when I finally do, caving inward. A surge of pride runs through me. *I* did that. I do have control here. I can give this man—my mate—what he wants.

I stroke gently at first and Rex hums with approval. "Don't be scared, Imogene. I won't break."

I tighten my grip, stroking up and down, feeling the velvet covering the hard shaft. His breathing changes, deeper—louder. His fingers on one hand twist in the blanket, but his other hand finds the back of my neck, the nape, and he tugs at my hair.

"That's good, baby," he grunts. "God, your hands are so soft."

My stomach flip flops, burning desire building at my core. If he touched me right now, I think I'd let him. Let him draw me to the edge and fulfill my own needs. He doesn't, he just watches me with those piercing blue eyes, jaw tensing as I grip him harder, tugging until there's nothing but blistering hard heat.

"Fuck," he grunts, body growing rigid. "Fuck, I'm gonna—"

White semen spills from the tip, hot and drippy over my fist. As he seizes, pulling hard at my hair, I remember the taste, the salty fluid. There's a craving to taste it again, but I focus now on not making a mess. On making sure he's fulfilled. I hold firm, not releasing him until I've milked every last drop.

He falls back against the pillow, releasing my hair. His chest covered in a thin sheen of sweat.

"Damn," he sighs, hand running through his hair. "Guess I should thank Silas for that, huh?"

Or me, I think, but bite it back. No. It's not about me. It's about him. And if anyone should be thanked, it's the women from the gathering last night. They are the ones that gave me the courage to take this step.

"I hope that was good enough," I say, grabbing a section of the sheet to clean up. I wait to see if he's going to say more, but when I look up from the mess, his eyes have fluttered shut and his chest has the rise and fall of a sleeping, satisfied man.

I'm on the way to the Center when I notice the construction. I'd taken a different route, stopping by the butcher to request an order for dinner that night. The small shop is two blocks over from the community center and there's a scenic route I sometimes like to take to the gate out of Serendee. The land is unused and a bit isolated, spotted with pines. Now it's been cleared, the ground has been churned up and flattened into a smooth surface of red clay. Large dirt moving machines are scattered across the field— community members on the construction team are busy at work.

I pause, staring at the space, wondering if I missed some announcement or news. Usually, construction or buildings are presented during one of Anex's talks. Was I too distracted by my circumstances to notice? Did it come out during the lecture when I sat in Rex's lap, and he pushed his hands between my legs?

It's after I've walked away that I see a familiar face. Clarissa, the woman that supervised my Domum, is coming down the road. Her expression brightens when she sees me and we rush together in greeting.

"Imogene," she says, "you look well."

"Thank you, as do you."

Clarissa looks the same as always. Modest blue dress, hair swept behind her head in a tight bun. She's single—and revealed to me that Anex never gave her an Order. She's wise and understands Serendee in a way I don't think I fully comprehended when we shared a home.

The sound of a machine moving draws my attention back down the hill. "I didn't know they were building," I say, admitting my possible Lapse. "Do you know what it is?"

"Anex hasn't officially announced it yet," she says, giving me relief that I'm not completely clueless. "But," she lowers her voice even though no one is around, "it's going to be a new childcare center."

"A childcare center?"

"Yes, for infants and toddlers. An opportunity to reach the youngest members of our community—sharing The Way as early as possible."

This is new. Children born into Serendee stay at home with their mothers or fathers or maybe are watched by a relative or neighbor. It's one of the foundations of the community—slowing down, making time to raise children in The Way. There has never been any kind of formal care for the smallest members of the community. But I can see the need. As the community grows, so do our obligations and time commitment.

"Anex asked me to help set it up." Clarissa beams, clearly proud of the assignment. "He recognized the success I've had with the girls living in the Domum."

I grin back. "That's an honor, but not a surprise, not with your years of service to the community." She blushes, something I'm not sure I've ever seen her do before. "I can't wait to see what you come up with."

"It's become his number one priority," she says. "I think that's why he hasn't announced it yet publicly. He's just moving fast, but you know how he is when he's excited about a new project."

She's right. Anex gets a vibration about him when he's in the middle of something new—something *great*—for the community.

We part, my heart feeling even lighter than before. Progress is being made in Serendee. Our leader is expanding and focused on the future. It's a wonderful time to live here.

That's the attitude I take with me back to the Center. A hum of excitement running through my blood. It's time for me to do my part. To ready myself for Enlightenment.

It's time for Correction.

9

———

L evi

"SHE CAME TO YOU AGAIN, didn't she?" Anex asks. There's no question about who 'she' is. There's only one she. "Seeking Correction?"

I didn't tell him when he called us in for the meeting, unsure of how to handle Imogene's need for discipline and the information about the women's group. He figured it out anyway. I guess there was a part of me that had hoped she would come to my room again and let me meter out punishment there in the privacy of my bedroom. I should've known Anex was aware. He's always aware.

"Yes. Just like you said, despite all the conflict and Rex filling her mind with questions, she's on the path. She craves discipline."

He gestures to the door in the back hallway of The Center, and I follow him down to the basement. We stop in the small area adjacent to the main room. Imogene should be here any minute for our scheduled session.

"Good." He walks over to a cabinet hanging from the wall. "I know this has been challenging for your Levi. Rex is testing your loyalty to both him and The Way. It's a hard place to exist—harder on you than it is on Elon or Silas. You've always been so devoted and followed my teachings as closely as possible. I know what I'm asking of you has been hard."

"I understand," I tell him. "I trust your judgment. The number one goal is to keep Rex in Serendee, and so far, we've accomplished that."

"We have." He smiles and I can't help the surge of pride in my chest. Praise and favor from Anex are all I've ever longed for. Even now, caught in this web between him and his son, the feeling emerges. "As long as we keep him and Imogene moving forward, I have faith Rex will come to his senses."

"And Imogene?" I ask, not meaning to. "What happens to her in the end?"

He looks thoughtful for a moment, but says, "Imogene has always been on a unique path—almost like she's been on a special journey. One that has led her to this point. What happens to her next is up to her, Rex and all of you assisting her."

Ah. There it is. The subtle threat that underlines all of Anex's directives. Do as I say. Follow the rules. Make me happy. And if you do those things, everything will be okay. If not?

Well, it's not a risk I'm willing to take.

He opens up the cabinet door and attached to the wall are a variety of instruments—all used during Correction. I've been trained to use many of these and watch as he removes a brown leather strap off of one of the hooks.

My heart skips a beat when I see it, but I keep my emotions close. I learned a long time ago that if Anex sees a reaction, he files it away for later. He holds it up. "I think she's ready."

I'm not so sure about that.

A knock on the outer door cuts our conversation short, and I enter the basement, leaving him. I keep my eyes away from the framed artwork on the wall—the image of Serendee. A sun moon and crown combination. Nearly every room in Serendee is monitored. This one is no different.

I rest the strap on the table in the center of the room and then open the door. Imogene stands on the other side, her expression innocent, but I see the spark of fire in her eyes. She craves these sessions, the feeling of surrendering herself to pain while seeking the pathway to redemption. A flicker of energy thrums between us that neither of us acknowledges. She steps into the room, the scent of her shampoo wafting behind her, and I try not to think about what it was like to have my nose buried into it while she leaned against me, and Silas buried himself between her legs.

I shut the door, making sure it's secure. "Do you want to tell me why you're here today?"

She stops in front of the table centered in the room and stares at the strap. Her skin pales and her fingers twist together. I see the long swallow in her throat and the way she forces her eyes away from the instrument, to look at me. "I stole and ate half a cake during Anex's birthday celebration," she starts, as if the Lapses can't help but fall from her tongue. "I tried not to eat today, but I felt lightheaded."

"You've been given permission to expand your caloric intake," I remind her. "And I suspect stealing that cake was more Rex's idea that yours."

"It's my job to keep him on the path."

"It's your job to keep him in Serendee. Focused. You did that." I cross my arms over my chest. "If that's all you're coming to me with, you probably should leave."

It's a ploy, of course, a way to get her to tell me more—confess to deeper Lapses. I wonder if she'll tell me about the women's meeting, if she'll betray the secret she promised to uphold?

"You're going to make me say it?" Her accusation is thick. "Even though you were there?"

I hold her eye. "Part of the process is admitting the Lapse. No one can own that but you."

"Fine," she says defiantly. "I had sex with a man that is not my future mate. I kissed another man. I received pleasure from a third." The look she gives me is pointed—accusing. "And then when my Ordered came to claim me I fought him off." Her chin lifts. "Is that enough?"

"It should be." I cross my arms over my chest. "But even with those Lapses, I'm not sure I should be correcting you now that you and Rex have bonded. Things have changed."

A small tremor runs through her. She wants the Correction. Even if she hasn't done anything to deserve it—she *needs* it. "Rex has given his explicit permission for us to continue our... relationships. Approved or not, it's wrong. I know it in my soul."

And there it is. That's what sent her here. Rex uses her for his own needs and then tosses her to the wolves like scraps of meat.

"Please, Levi." Her voice is soft, barely audible. "I need this."

The truth is that I was always going to give her what she wanted. It's my job to make her work for it—to suffer through the moment. Enlightenment doesn't come easy. Not for any of us.

I give her a small nod and command, "Lift your skirt and bend over the desk."

Relief rushes out of her, and she reaches under her skirt. Hopping on one foot, she removes a pair of white, lace, panties and rests them on the table. Her hands shake as she gathers the fabric, balling it around her waist. She knows the position: bent over, hands flat on the table, backside propped up and exposed. I'm hard before she bares herself, the smooth, pale, flesh healed from our last session. I know she's already warm between her legs and soon she'll be slippery and wet.

This is as much of a test for me as it is to her. I reach around her, grabbing the strap. The leather is cool and smooth in my hand, similar to her pale backside. I run my hand over the skin, gentle, getting a feel for her supple flesh. My heart pounds as I grip the strap in my fingers, knowing this girl has done nothing to deserve this type of punishment, yet also very aware that she's been conditioned to want it.

Just as I've been conditioned to give it.

I swing my arm back and strike her against her backside, my teeth grinding from the force. The power surges her forward and a small cry escapes her mouth. Hearing that sound brings up a swell of desire, but I swallow it back. This session is about training Imogene, not fulfilling my needs, and although we crossed that line once, it was in the dark hours of the night, in our home. Not here.

Not with Anex watching.

10

———

I mogene

THE FINAL STING of the strap barely filters through the fog that has lowered over my brain. The first jolt was severe, a sensation I've never experienced. I felt like my skin had been cracked open by a shock of lightening. Tears streamed down my cheeks, and I fought a wave of nausea. I almost begged him to stop.

Almost.

I asked for this. Wanted it, and despite the fact that my backside became numb after the fifth slap of leather, the warm familiar spread of heat built in my stomach, desperate and hungry. Levi is diligent with his Correction. The strikes coming in a consistent measure. He throws his whole body into it, and I feel the force all the way down to my toes. My body surges forward with each hit, knees shaking, until I'm nearly flat on the table, unable to move.

I take it, knowing I deserve it, but there's a tingle under my skin because what I truly want comes next. I wait for the escalation, the heavy breathing, the touch of his hands between my legs, the sound of Levi's zipper lowering, and the final rush of transcendent euphoria.

It never comes and neither, to my surprise, does he.

I glance over my shoulder and see Levi's sweaty, pinched, face. He looks disgusted. With me? With himself? As I struggle to an upright position he walks toward the door. "You're leaving?" I ask, feeling more exposed than during my Correction. I grip the table with one hand and squeeze my thighs together in a futile attempt to quell the urges.

"We're done here." He shifts with discomfort, the bulge of his erection obvious. "Clean up and leave when you've composed yourself."

My brain is still a fog, caught up in the blistering numbness of my backside and the ache between my legs and I watch as he exits. The door shutting with a click behind him.

I don't know if I should be angry or hurt. Maybe neither? What I know is that I'm flustered and in pain. Throbbing, inside and out. I do know that if he's left the room, then so should I.

I lower my skirt and smooth the wrinkled fabric with shaking hands. My panties, which were on the table, are gone now. That makes two pairs Levi has taken. I can't help but wonder what he does with them.

When I get myself to point of control, I take a hesitant step outside. The summer sky is bright, the birds are flittering in the nearby trees. Things are normal out here, the direct opposite of the room I just left. My skin feels raw and my senses are still numb, I'm distracted—deep in my thoughts—when a figure steps in my path.

"Oh." I blink. "Elon? What are you—"

There's no reason to finish the question. I know why he's here and he knows why I'm here.

"Do you need something?" I ask. "I was just on my way—"

"No, Little Lamb, I don't need anything," his eyes skim my body, like he can see through the fabric of my dress, "but I think you do."

"Excuse me?" I look around. This is not a topic for a public area. "I don't know what you're talking about."

He grabs my hand. "You're shaking."

"Because I shouldn't be seen with a man that isn't my betrothed." I try to twist away from him, but his grip is firm. "Let me go before we both get in trouble."

"Why? The more trouble you get in, the more Corrections you can have. Isn't that what you want?"

His presence is powerful and intimidating, but his knowledge is worse. It's wrong for me to push back and question him, but my heart is still racing from the emotional and physical overload of the Correction, and I'm not sure I can handle this. Not now. Not with him.

"I want what I always want—to seek Enlightenment. To squash indulgence. To do better."

"I think you want something else, Imogene." My real name coming off his tongue feels even more threatening—more intimate. His hand runs down my back. I brace myself and when he touches my raw backside, I hiss. He bends down and whispers in my ear, "A little sore?"

"I'm fine." In a fast movement he grabs me under the legs and picks me up. "What are you doing! What if someone sees!"

"No one will see," he assures me.

A six-foot-four man, carrying another man's future mate around Serendee like a bag of flour. Someone *will* notice. I fight against him, but it's useless. My energy is zapped, my backside screams in pain, and he's just too big.

"Are you taking me to Silas again?" I ask, hopefully.

"No, his salves won't fix this." He turns back to the door and props me against his knee while he presses the code into the door. The lock unlatches, and he steps inside where he drops me in front of the table I'd just been bending over. The strap lies where Levi left it. He stares at it for long moment and then says, "I'm here to finish what Levi started."

My heart leaps from my chest to my throat. "You're going to punish me more?"

Levi's strikes had been strong and powerful, but Elon... he'd break me.

"No. This isn't about punishment. It's about giving you what you really want." He yanks up my skirt, exposing my blistering behind. The cool air feels good on the raw skin and against the searing heat between my legs. His voice is low in my ear, "This pain... it's just an excuse to take you where you want to go. I don't like to see you hurt like this." His finger gently runs over the welts. I flinch, but he holds me still. "I know what you need and how you need it."

I have no time to think about what Elon is demanding of me, because he grabs my waist and spins me around, pushing my hips into the table. The legs scrape against the cement floor, but all I hear is the sound of his zipper lowering.

My belly bottoms out when I feel his erection slide between my legs, sending a shiver of relief down my spine. "Tell me this isn't exactly what you came here for, Little Lamb, and I'll stop."

All arguments die on my tongue because the feel of him next to me, slippery and wet, *is* exactly what I want. It's all I think about. It's all I crave. Levi lit a fire in me and left it smoldering. Elon's stoked it back to life and as his hand presses into the curve of my lower back, I beg, "Don't."

"Don't what?"

"Don't stop." Then I add, "Make it hurt."

His fingers twist in my hair, and I cry out when he yanks against my scalp. "Like this?"

"Yes." The answer turns into a hiss when his hand brushes against my swollen, sore backside, but it just adds to the intensity of the moment. The sheer, uncontrollable want that surges through me.

"All of those other sessions have built up to this." His cock rubs against me, the tip pushing and prodding at my folds. "Levi is too good, too righteous to take it where it needs to go. Where *you* need it to go."

He grabs me by the neck and twists my mouth up to his. His lips are scorching, his tongue demanding. I pant into his mouth, and he says, "But I'm not. I'm just the kind of man to give you what you deserve."

He drops my head and grips my hip, pushing into me with a hard thrust. I slam forward, caught by surprise by the feel of the force of him inside of me. He's big, thick, and he pushes against my sides. He's intrusive, invading, and although he gives me a second to catch my breath the second punch is just as forceful—if not more. He slams into me, fingers pinching into my hips. Every time he does it, pushing to the hilt, my backside sings from the contact— a constant reminder of my Lapses. With every thrust, I just keep adding them.

"Tell the truth," he says, voice tight, "you want this. You want it dirty and hard and primal."

"N-no." I stutter, the word thrust out of me. "I want Enlightenment."

My head snaps back with a sharp yank of my hair. "You want to be fucked. You want your pussy so full of my cum that it'll be dripping down your legs when it's over."

I fight back—trying to stay focused, even as he thrusts into me, nerves frayed. "I seek pain to fight the Indulgence of an easy path."

The phrases come so easily. They're rote. Ingrained in me since childhood.

"Bullshit," he growls, jerking me up and pinching my nipples roughly. A shock of desire travels straight between my legs, and his hands follow the current, stopping at my core. "It's okay to want it because you like it. You like it when I touch you here and fuck you at the same time."

I swallow an affirmation. It's wrong. Nothing in my life is about what I want. I've been taught that from the beginning. I didn't grow up in the same world as Elon, where gluttony is rewarded with rolled up money and fast cars. Where women give sex freely without consequences and guilt.

"I want you to come for me, Little Lamb. For *me*. Not for Anex. Not for The Way. Not for Rex." He leans over me, bodies pressed together. He's moving deliciously slow now, dragging his cock in and out. My legs wobble, and he holds me up. "I want you to do it for me because you like how it feels when I'm buried deep inside you. When you can't tell where you begin, and I end."

God, he feels so good. So sinfully good. A tremor rolls through me and I fight it. "It's wrong."

"Is it?" His breath is hot on the back of my neck, his body slick with sweat. I feel the cascade building, intensifying with every press of his fingertips, every stab of his cock. He's right. I don't know where I begin, and he ends. I don't know anything other than it hurts so good. "Come for me," he urges. "Just for me."

"I can't."

"You can and you will."

He's right, of course, my body has a will of its own and all it wants is release. His fingers rub circles against my clit, and I groan, overwhelmed by so much stimulation. The first twinges come quick, and the orgasm rushes over me, down my arms and legs, spreading from my core up my spine. My body grows numb, lost in the luxury of euphoria, and Elon picks up his pace, flattening me on the table. Every thrust sends another shockwave across my body. Part pain, part desire, all of it lost to the feeling of him thrusting so deep.

"That's right," he mutters, voice rough and caught between ragged breaths. "Clench around me. Hold on tight." I don't know how long he'll go, and I feel a second wave of want tickling at the base of my spine. Abruptly, he comes to a halt, jerking into me with a groan as his cock swells thick. We stay like this for a long moment, his seed spilling into me, my muscles milking every last drop. Slowly, I float back down into my body, and he pulls out. I push up on my elbows and stand, feeling his cum drip down my inner thigh.

I panic, looking for something to clean up with, but he drops to his knees and pulls a handkerchief out of his back pocket. Before I can stop him, he gently wipes away the evidence of his transgressions.

He stands and looks at me, eyes less rageful than I've ever seen. I almost thank him, but for what? Cleaning me up? Nearly forcing himself on me? Pushing me to my limits?

The words falter on my tongue because I'm not entirely convinced that what just transpired between us wasn't the biggest Lapse of my life, or if it was exactly the level of Enlightenment I've been seeking.

"From now on you either tell Levi what you really want from these sessions, or you come to me. Or if you're that desperate," he grins, zipping up his pants, "come to us both. Understand?"

Both? That idea shocks me to move, and despite my wrinkled dress and messy hair, I rush out the door. Thank God, no one is around as I limp back toward Serendee. I pretend I'm a normal woman, going back to my normal home, with my normal mate waiting for me. I pretend that Elon's fluids aren't wet between my legs, and Levi's strap marks aren't blistered on my backside and that I haven't just willingly participated in something I don't fully understand.

The only thing I do know is that for the first time in days I feel satisfied, physically and emotionally, which either means I'm on the right path, or headed down a very, very, wrong one.

11

R^{ex}

THE EXCHANGE TAKES place in the back entrance of the Lambda fraternity house. The crates lined with bricks of weed, then covered in soft packing material. On top is an assortment of fresh fruit and vegetables. The truck I'm driving today is rusted out and looks like something that belongs on a farm, the faded Serendee logo on the side. It's all part of the image: organic and wholesome, yet pull back a few layers, and the truth is exposed.

"Thanks, man," Mac says, handing me the envelope of cash. "We've got a big party coming up this weekend. We need to *feed* a lot of people."

Mac's a big guy—looks like he spends more time in the gym than in class—but what do I know? My father limited my education to the classes available on Serendee plus his own lectures. I guess he did give me a big dose of economics, too: supply and demand.

There's a reason he picked weed as his primary product. Our community is adjacent to a notorious party school.

"Happy to do business with you," I say, opening the creaky, rusty door. "I think you'll be very happy with our... produce."

"Hey," he calls as I step inside. "You should come by the party this weekend. Bring some friends."

"Thanks, I'll swing by if I have time."

I get in the truck and crank the engine. This is how it works. Serendee grows the product, I deliver it, posing like I'm just a regular guy, and I get an invite. Then I start recruiting for more sales and yeah, marks for my dad.

He only wants the rich ones—preferably women, but he'll take a few men. He needs able bodies to do the grunt work down at the farm or around the community. Turning out of the frat house driveway, I take a left, riding through campus. I check the time. The hand off went pretty quickly, which gives me time for another stop.

I find a spot to park on the street and head up the big set of stairs toward the University library. Inside I go straight to the bank of computers, passing clusters of students on their laptops or at tables surrounded by books. It's not hard to fit in. I'm the right age and know how to acclimate—another one of my father's traits that I inherited. Most of it is about confidence, just *thinking* you belong. Knowing it. I pass a group of chairs where a girl in a short skirt looks up and gives me a flirty smile. I return it, but keep walking, sliding into one of the privacy corrals. I take one more discrete look around, before getting online. I never can be sure, but I don't think Anex has any spies in here.

I have an entire series of accounts that I only use when my father can't see them. Although the rest of Serendee shuns electronics, the Chosen have access to pretty much whatever we want. He talks a big game about not rotting your mind with secular devices, but he knows how the world works. You can't rule it without high-speed fiber and access to offshore banking.

I start how I always do, pulling up the file I've collected on my mother, Beatrice Wray. Sometimes her maiden surname, Holt.

Nothing much comes up, a few articles about the beginning of Serendee. I bring up one article that I've read a dozen times. It's from the University paper, talking about a group of students with an inspiring project; the development of a self-sustaining community. It's mostly my father's early ramblings, about fresh air and food, equality and getting back to basics. It's long before he took on his iconic role of the leader in the community. Back when his name was Tim Wray, before he took the title of Anex.

There's one quote from my mother. "I look forward to living in a safe, supportive community, free of the disparity and corruption of society."

"Safe," I mutter, shaking my head. "You married a sociopath. There's not much safe about that."

I flip over to the medical examiner's report—Beatrice died at home, a blood clot exploding in her brain. I've skimmed this paper a hundred times, but I don't believe it. I was fourteen when she died, and I felt the change in her long before that. I saw her nervous smile and heard the whispered arguments between her and my father. He'd started implementing the Domums. He'd changed his name. All eyes were on him—not the community as a whole. Guards were placed around the borders, and the barn was under construction. He had plans for Serendee and my mother didn't agree with them.

How lucky for him that she died during this tension and turmoil. And, I think, looking at the bottom of the report at the medical examiner's signature—Virginia Bloom. How lucky is it for him to have the doctor that signed this paper to now be a member and his personal healer in Serendee?

I pull up the internet browser, taking the steps to open my social media accounts. They're under false names—as much to hide them from my father as from anyone looking into our business dealings. I like friend contacts in the secular world—the frat boys and people I meet at the club. I've also found my mother's long defunct account. I can see her profile, but it's limited. The photos are old—she'd stopped using it when they moved to

Serendee, back when it was more of a campground than a commune. Just the fact she kept it up feels like an act of defiance to my father—something that makes me feel closer to her. It's useless to me though. What I need is to get into the actual account, but I have no idea what email she used or her password.

I stare at the computer for a long time, frustration building. This is where I always hit a brick wall. How can I prove what my father did if everyone believes his lies? If the medical examiner is covering his tracks? On her page, I click on the different tabs. Photos: just old profile pictures. Information: blank. Friends: the list is short, but it pops up. I scan down the page.

A face pops out at me, and I pause, feeling a hollowing out in my stomach. The name, Camille Sanders means nothing to me, but the face... I know it. I've seen those lips pull back in a nervous smile and the eyes widen with fear.

That face—or a younger version of it—belongs to Imogene. My mate.

Imogene wasn't at The Center when I stopped to look for her. Another girl sat behind the desk, gawking at me and mumbling about how she wasn't feeling well and went home. I drive back to Serendee. In general vehicles aren't allowed outside of the garage and work areas, but I'm too impatient to stop, pulling the old truck in front of our cottage.

I've just closed the front door when Silas walks out of the downstairs bathroom, holding something in his hands.

"Where is she?" I ask.

"Upstairs, but—"

I don't wait for an answer and take the stairs two at a time. I've always known about Imogene's mother—the Regressive. She'd been removed years before for her destructive thoughts and attitude. I've never really thought about where she is now, or the fact she knew my mother. Maybe she can tell me more about what I'm looking for.

I enter our bedroom without knocking, prepared to rouse Imogene to tell me what knows. She's asleep. Flat on her stomach. I move to wake her when I hear, "Don't. She needs her rest."

I spin and see Silas in the doorway. "What gives you the right to tell me how to handle my mate?"

"The fact she stumbled in here, barely able to walk two hours ago."

"What are you talking about?" I frown and look down at her. Nothing about her looks unusual other than her position. Every other time I've seen her asleep, she's been curled up on her side. "What's wrong with her?"

I don't wait for an answer, yanking back the quilt covering her body. She's wearing a cotton nightgown, but it's pushed up to her waist. Her ass is blistered, flaming red.

"She went for Correction," Silas says. "Things got... a little rough. I gave her a pill and applied some salve. It worked last time, but the wounds weren't so severe."

"Last time? Who did this?" Wild rage burns in my chest. I spin and look at Silas. "Was it my father?"

"No," he replies, but I see the flicker of apprehension in his eyes. "She chose this, Rex. It's part of the philosophy. You know that."

"This," I say, turning to look back at the bloody welts and bruises, "is my father's fucked up mind games. It's how he controls." I step toward him. "I'll ask again and I expect an answer. Who did this?"

Silas isn't as tall as I am but he's broad shouldered and not intimidated by me. He glances over at Imogene before grabbing me by the shirt and drags me into the hall.

"You're right. She's a creation of your father's just like the rest of us. Correction is part of her life—it's how she copes. You can't blame her Guide. It's not like you're around here to take care of her."

My hands ball into fists, but I don't hit him, I just push past him down the hall and fling open Elon and Levi's doors. Neither are inside, but just seeing Levi's room, the books and journals tells me everything I need to know. Levi will do *anything* my father asks, including damaging my property.

"Where is he?"

He swallows. "Don't make this harder than it already is", he says.

I run my hands through my hair, tugging at the ends. "Where the fuck is he?"

The door slams downstairs and rage fuels me down the stairs. Levi stands in the hallway, hanging his satchel on a hook on the wall. I rush him, plowing my hands into his chest and smashing him into the wooden door.

"What the hell?" he shouts, eyes wide with shock. He struggles against me, but I leverage my forearm against his chest to keep him pinned.

"I saw what you did to her. She's torn up and bloody!"

"I'm her Guide," he says, without an inch of remorse. "She asked for Correction."

"And you beat her black and blue?"

"She—"

"No! No excuses. I've given a lot of leniency when it comes to her and you three, but destroying my property isn't one of them."

The backdoor flings open and Elon walks in. He takes in the two of us and exhales. "What is this?"

"Levi Corrected Imogene," Silas says. "Rex has suddenly decided he's the only one that can play with his toy."

I spin around. "Shut up."

The distraction is enough for Levi to shove me off and get around me. He stands next to Elon and rubs his chest. "Tell him," Levi says, looking at Elon. "Tell him about his Ordered."

There's something about Elon's expression I can't read. Something conflicted yet knowledgeable. "Tell me what?"

"She wants it like that," he says. "Needs it. Rough and painful. Anex has gotten in her head. She's so fucked up and twisted she can't tell pleasure from pain. So, when she's confused or feels guilty she goes to him."

My eyes dart to Levi. "And you what? Fuck her?"

"I *Correct* her. That's all." But I see it in his eyes. That's not all he does to her.

"He's telling the truth," Elon says, crossing his arms over his chest. "I saw her after. She could barely function."

"Because he tore the skin off her ass."

"Because he left her hanging. She was sloppy wet, cunt swollen and aching. She couldn't see straight."

"So what? You brought her home and let Silas put her to bed?"

"No," he shakes his head, without a trace of remorse. "I gave her what she needed. I fucked the guilt and pain out of her. I fucked her pussy so hard that all of this bullshit was gone—your rejection, your father's manipulation, her worry about Lapses." I start to argue but he holds up his hand. "Before you start about how you're not like your father, just stop. You're not any better. Taking her virginity like that. Going in at night and showing up when you feel like it. She'll do anything to please you. Take any abuse."

"Don't you dare compare us."

"He's not," Silas says, jumping in, "but you need to pay attention, brother. She's lost. Confused. Caught up in a world we've dragged her into. One that you keep threatening to leave, and one in which your father will then remain, ready to snatch her up when you go.

"I'm here, aren't I?"

But the statement falls flat. I'm here because I needed something from *her*. I wasn't there when she needed guidance. When she needed a cock buried deep inside to relieve the pain. Or later when she needed someone to soothe her wounds.

I take, I don't give. Fucking hell, I am like my goddam father.

"I don't know how to give her what she needs. That's not who I am," I admit.

"See, that's the thing," Silas says, clapping me on the back, "we do. We need to build her up, keep her strong, and show her that we can take care of her."

"And my father? Let's not pretend you aren't all working directly for him."

"We do this like we do everything," Elon says, "one foot in and one out of the system. He taught us this world, Rex, but he also gave us something he didn't anticipate."

I raise an eyebrow. "What's that?"

"Power."

12

———

I mogene

I WAKE to the bed shifting, the weight of a person next to me. I'm still on my stomach, backside aching, but turn my head to see the person next to me. Silas.

"Good morning," he says, pushing the hair off my neck. "How did you sleep?"

"Okay, I guess. I tried rolling over a few times." I make a face. "Didn't work so well."

He holds up a small pot. "I brought some salve. It'll help heal the wounds and swelling. May I?"

I nod, eager for some relief. Things got a little extreme with Levi the day before. Something intense came over me. Like a craving for water on a hot day. I didn't just want him to Correct me like that, I needed it to survive. That doesn't even include what happened with Elon afterward.

Silas gently lowers the blanket and pushes up my nightdress

allowing the cool air to hit my backside. I watch his face as he does it, the wrinkle in his nose at the sight of the injury.

"Is it bad?" I ask.

"I've seen worse."

That surprises me. Almost as much as the sensation I feel when his fingers make contact with my flesh, rubbing the cool, icy feeling salve over my blistered skin. "Oh! That's nice."

"Good." He smiles. "I made it last night. I knew you needed something a little more potent than my normal cream."

I relax into the massage, enough that I build the courage to ask, "What did you mean when you said you've seen worse?"

He dips his fingers in the pot, scooping out a glob. "Part of my job is to treat wounds like this. I'm not a healer—well not the medical kind—I'm more about treating the soul, the sexual one, and sometimes that pent up frustration results in physical injury. Like yours."

He continues to massage, moving away from the blisters, down over the curve of my backside, until he dips his fingers between the crack. My belly flutters, twisting with that familiar desire. This one is less conflicted though. It's nice. Wanting. Relaxing.

"Do you think I'm crazy for letting Levi do this to me?" I ask when his fingers travel up my back.

"I think you're seeking The Way—Enlightenment. That doesn't come without sacrifice."

"Have you ever done something like this?" I watch his face when I ask. "To yourself or others?"

"I've experienced the strap," he says, the corners of his mouth tugging down. "But it's not my thing. I love skin and flesh. I like it soft and whole. I want to taste it, lick it, kiss it, treasure it." His eyes meet mine. "I'm not judging. But I prefer to push myself and the people I work with to the edge in a different manner. Less painful. More transcendent."

As he explains this, his hands wander, gently stroking my skin. He explores every inch, the soft parts under my arms, or the slight curve along the side of my breasts. It tickles and nags, pulling at a string coiled tightly at my belly. Heat builds on my skin, a contrast from the cool salve Silas coated over my wounds.

"There's more than one way to reach Enlightenment," he says, pushing my cheeks apart and running his finger down to the tight ring. "Do you want to experience it?"

My body jerks in surprise, but that is followed by a spreading warmth under my skin. It pulses in my veins. I have no idea what he's asking of me, but I trust this man. He's done nothing but keep me safe and healthy. "Please," I breathe. "It's all I want."

He removes his hands and retrieves a different bottle. He wipes the salve off his fingertips and coats them in a slippery oil. He returns to his work, massaging the underside of my butt cheeks. The pressure is deep, assuring, and by the time he returns to the puckered ring my body is wracked with desire. Silas teases around the edge and whispers in my ear, "Relax, Imogene, you'll feel a little pressure at first, but I'll go slow."

I take a deep breath and just as I release it, he pushes his finger inside. My belly twists and my muscles tighten.

"Ease up, or it'll hurt."

What Silas doesn't know is that pain doesn't scare me, but even I can sense my tension is keeping him out. I inhale again and he pushes inside, stretching me as he goes. "How does that feel?"

"Strange?" He curves his finger a little and a shiver runs down my spine. "Good. Oh, yes, good."

He settles into a gentle rhythm, stretching me from the inside out. There's discomfort, but it's different. It's not tied up in conflict. It's just my body acclimating to something new—something exciting.

Silas's free hand shifts, and I feel the flutter of his fingertips along the nerves at the front of my body. They're slippery and slick, coating the hot bundle at the crux of my body. I suck in a gasp, bucking forward and back. To feel Silas inside and out like this, it sends shockwaves through my body, each one escalating as it builds toward the strong force that overtakes me.

"That's it," Silas says, bending to kiss me. "Ride it out."

The orgasm wracks through me, and I close my eyes, panting through the experience. It's not until my body stills, and Silas has removed his fingers, that I open my eyes and realize we're not alone. I jolt up, fearful. "I—"

Rex's eyes are blazing, his mouth set in a thin line. "Clean yourself up and get dressed. We need to talk."

He walks out before I can react, and I look to Silas who is still beside me. "Is he upset?"

"It's hard to know lately. He's on edge."

"Will he be upset that you did that to me? That I allowed you to do it?"

"He gave us permission, remember?" Silas brushes my hair off my face and helps me to an upright position. The pain in my backside feels better. "And I doubt he's mad. Probably jealous."

I snort. "I doubt that."

He shrugs and kisses me gently on the mouth. "It's good that he's here and wants to see you. Get ready. I'll tell him you'll be out soon."

I take my time, washing up and braiding my hair. I pull on one of my every day dresses, the fabric made from hemp cultivated on site and dyed with natural colorings. By the time I go to the living room, walking gingerly, he's there alone. His eyes sweep over me, most likely resentful of my choice in clothing.

"Sorry I took so long. Can I get you something to eat or drink?"

He nods at the chair. "Sit."

I ease into the chair, trying not to grimace as the pain swells. I place my hands in my lap and wait for what's coming; punishment, admonishment, abuse. With Rex it could be anything.

"I want to talk to you about your mother."

I blink, trying to process his words. "My mother?"

He nods. "Yes. I know she and my mother were friends."

Heat prickles at my neck. Speaking of my mother... it's not completely forbidden but it's frowned upon. It puts a target on my back by making people remember what happened when she rejected Serendee and Anex's ways. She's Regressive and was banished from the community.

"I'm sure that was before my mother made her thoughts and feelings known. I doubt Beatrice would have allowed herself to be tarnished by someone so—"

"Stop." He says. I gape for a moment, then swallow. "You shouldn't feel shame about your mother. God, she's probably the only person that lived here that I respect."

"Excuse me?"

"She had the guts to stand up to my father. She fought for her beliefs." He sets his eyes on me. "The only thing I blame her for is leaving you here."

I stare at him, my heart thudding in my chest. No one has said anything positive about my mother in years. Her name is uttered as a curse—a warning, but here is the second most powerful man in Serendee telling me that he respects her. As much as he can respect any female.

As much as I'd like to bask in it, paranoia creeps up my spine. "We shouldn't talk about this."

"See," he runs his hand through his fair hair, "that's what they tell you to keep us from developing our own ideas. To keep us from the truth. If topics are forbidden then we won't ask questions and look for answers."

"What answer do you want?" I ask, feeling the edge of anxiety building. "What possibly can you want to know that involves my mother?"

He leans forward and I catch a hint of his warm, clean scent. It's alluring and disarming. "I want to find her, Little Lamb, and I want you to help me."

13

I mogene

Rex's request hangs over me like a cloak of paranoia as I go about my work. Part of living in Serendee is never feeling alone. We're a community. We live together, eat together, work together. Eyes are always on us, but it's for our own good. It's how we work to Be Better, knowing someone else is keeping us accountable.

The other things: the training, the extra calories, the bras and panties I wear under my standard dresses, those happen behind closed doors. But looking for my mother's contact information? That requires stealth and sneakiness.

Rex doesn't tell me where to look, but I have a good idea of a place to start: The Center.

I arrive early. The only other business open is the coffee shop two doors down. I keep my chin level, forcing myself not to look at the ground or appear suspicious in any way. It's silly, because no one notices me, but my heart still rattles in my chest as I open the front door and disengage the alarm.

I lock the door behind me, but don't turn on the light, then carry my belongings to my desk, putting everything away like normal.

I'm obeying my husband, I remind myself.

I am acting at his request.

I am fulfilling my duties as a mate.

This is what I tell myself as I walk down the back hallway to the records room. This room isn't a secret—the words are written on a plaque outside the door. Records. About every person that walks into this facility. Every person that lives in Serendee.

If there's information about Beatrice or my mother, it'll be in this room.

The problem is that no one is allowed in here without permission. I've only been in here twice, under the guidance of a male instructor who is tight in Anex's inner circle. I watched him punch in the code that day, and I stand before the keypad now, hoping it hasn't changed. Terrified that a slip up will alert someone to my presence.

I am fulfilling my duties as a mate.

I punch in the string of numbers I memorized. Why did I memorize them? Because that is who I am on a basic level, right? Tip toeing in the edge of Regressive. Defiant. Rebellious.

Inhaling sharply, I enter the last number and the keypad lights up, flashing green before the sound of the lock echoes in the empty hall. I enter before I can talk myself out of it and step into the room. It's the size of a classroom, each wall filled with file cabinets and four rows in between. I walk to the nearest one and pull out the drawer. Just as I remembered it is filled with file folders. Some thicker than others, but each with a name typed across the tab.

I pull out one and see the name Maribel Ashwood. Inside is a single sheet that has her age (19) Residence (Wittmore University) and the date she came in the Center. She took two classes but never returned. There's a picture of her stapled to the top, along with a few other details like her father's occupation, net worth and notes jotted by her instructor.

Looks like standard follow up methods were taken, but no one could get her to return. Right before I put her file away, I notice that her first meetings were two years ago. The last documentation on her though was three weeks ago. People are keeping tabs on her long after she lost interest.

The truth is that most people that walk into the Center don't join our ranks. They take a few classes, learn about Enlightenment but either can't afford to continue classes, or it's not a good fit. Not everyone is ready for this lifestyle.

I shut the cabinet door and move down the row, stopping at 'M.' I pull the drawer open and pick through the files. My stomach feels like a stampede of elephants is running through it, nausea rolling over me in waves. Once I open this wound, there's no going back. Not for Rex, not for me.

I am fulfilling my duties as a mate.

I stop at her name. Montgomery. There are three of us, my dad, my mom and me. My father's file is average for a man who has lived here his whole life. A history of his classes, job service, dedication. I don't waste time looking into it. Not now. My file is thick—twice the size of my father's which would have been surprising to me before my Ordering but not now. Anex would have documented every moment of my life once he found out his son wanted me for his mate.

It's tempting to see what it says about me, but a flash of the appointment with Anex's healer rushes to my mind, and I don't want to know. I'm barely able to make it through one day at a time now. To see it written on paper? I can't.

So I focus on the thinnest file of the three. Camille Sanders Montgomery. My heart sinks before I flip back the cover. It's too thin. Sure enough, there's a single sheet and a photo of my mother —young—right after college. The paperwork is succinct. Name, age, history, and a big red stamp across the page: Regressive.

The elephants in my belly vanish and are replaced with something else. Something I didn't know I was carrying until I saw the file.

Curiosity.

Real, genuine, curiosity.

Who is Camille Montgomery? Where is she? And why has Anex scrubbed her history?

I REALIZE LATER there is one person I can ask.

During my lunch break, I take the gravel road to the cluster of single person residences near the gym. Anex was an early adopter of small, environmentally sustaining homes. His theory is that people don't need to spend so much time isolated, not if they live in a strong community. Bathrooms and kitchens are part of a shared space in the center. My father has lived in one of these homes since my mother left, and I moved into the Domum.

I knock on the door knowing he should be home. I checked his work schedule before I left the office. I have access to everyone's daily schedule, and his said he was off today. As expected, it only takes him a moment to open the door. "Imogene," he says, his voice conveying his surprise. He recovers quickly, spreading his arms wide and giving me a hug. "How are you?"

"Good," I reply, allowing the gentle hug. My relationship with my father is superficial. The people of Serendee are my family. Anex my leader. Rex my mate. We both understand this. "How are you?"

"Wonderful." He gestures to the small front porch and we both take a seat on the ledge. "It's been a long time since you've visited," he says. "But I know you've been busy with your Order and the excitement of joining Anex's family."

He beams. It's a rare honor to become part of the inner circle. It reflects on him as well—just like it reflected on us when my mother was forced to leave. My current status elevates us both, which is why my coming here—and the reason behind it—is such a risk.

"It's definitely been a change," I say, smoothing out my dress. "Getting used to living with Rex has been eye opening." I give him a smile. "I'm sure you and mom went through your own challenges when you got married."

His grin slightly wavers. "That was a long time ago. It's hard to remember."

"I'm sure." I take a deep breath. "I need to ask you something."

"Anything, sweetheart. I owe you a betrothal gift."

"That isn't necessary." I look around, checking to make sure we're truly alone. All I hear is the birds chirping and the sounds of a tractor off in the distance. "Do you have a way to contact her?"

His head tilts. "Her?"

I hold his eye and a deep line forms on his forehead. "I don't know what you're talking about."

"Yes, you do, and I know it's an inappropriate topic, but I need to know."

He shakes his head, and I don't miss how his hands tremble. "Imogene, you've come farther than I ever expected with the mark of your mother's betrayal following you around. Why would you dig this up now?"

"It's important," I say, feeling the lump build in the pit of my stomach. "To me."

"No. Someone else is behind this." His voice is barely a whisper. I say nothing, just give him a hard look and he replies. "Anex? He wants this information? Is this a test? Is he questioning my loyalty?"

"No!" I say, too forcefully. A crow takes flight off the top of the community building. "No, daddy," I say, using the name from my childhood. "It isn't a test. Anex will never know. This is just between the two of us. I..." I swallow. "I'm about to mate with a powerful man and honestly, there are times in a woman's life where only one person can help her. I need my mother."

He takes my hand and squeezes it. The skin rougher than what I remember. "I can't help you, Imogene. And if you're smart you won't ask anyone else. If," he looks around, "if anyone hears of this, the consequences will be swift. Not even Rex will be able to help you."

It was a long shot, a stupid idea to come here. My mother wouldn't contact him anyway. My father is too weak. He doesn't carry the streak of defiance that runs through my blood—that clearly came from her.

"I understand," I say, rising. "I'm sorry if I upset you."

His blue eyes hold mine. "I'm sorry I couldn't give you what you wanted, but it's for your own good, sweetheart, I promise you."

I nod, taking a step away from the man I used to call my father. I realize now that whatever bond we shared back then is truly dissolved. Anex probably knew that the day he sent my mother away.

It's probably safer for both of us this way.

"It was good to see you, Imogene," he says, watching me walk away. "Be safe."

The last part is a warning, one that never would have been a problem—not until the day I was Ordered to marry Rex. I exit the housing area, headed back to the office, already trying to figure out the next step in fulfilling my mate's demands, no matter how risky they are.

When I returned to the office an envelope was leaning against my pencil cup. Inside are directions about the next women's meeting. Again, I'm to come alone, but this time not to the woods, but to Beatrice' house.

The house is dark, but the soft glow of candlelight flickers in the window. I enter and a note on the foyer table tells me to go to the second floor. The house is eerie like this, quiet and empty, but curiosity takes hold. This isn't just a house. It's Rex's childhood home. A shrine to his dead mother and family.

The instructions, set next to a lantern with a handle on top, say to go to the third door on the right, but I disobey, opening two others before I find the one I'm looking for. Rex's childhood bedroom. It, too, is set up like a museum: everything, from toys to photographs to the sports themed bedding, frozen in time.

I stop to look at a photograph of the family and hold up the light. Anex, Bea, and Rex, probably about six, posed outside on a beautiful fall day. Anex, who went by Tim before his wife died, is handsome, with warm sun-kissed skin and a wide smile. Beatrice is pretty—and I can see shades of both of them in their son. Rex stands between his parents on a brick wall, arms around their shoulders. I try to find hints of the man he is now, the man that spends his time tormenting me, but all I see is a sweet little boy.

I feel a tug of sorrow for the loss of him.

"There you are," a voice says, dragging me from my thoughts.

"Margaret." She's not hooded this time, although she's in dark clothes. I guess we're not hiding this time.

"Did you get turned around?" her question has a tone, one that implies that she knows I didn't misread the directions.

"Yes," I lie. "I was just so nervous; I didn't pay attention."

She takes my hand. "Don't be nervous. Tonight is about Enlightenment. When you walk out this door, you'll have the weight of womanhood lifted from your shoulders."

The weight of womanhood. Is that the cause for the noose around my neck? I follow Margaret to the room next door. It's the master bedroom. My spine goes rigid when I look behind the headboard. There's a painting—a portrait—of Anex. It's huge, framed in gold. He's sitting in on his lecture chair, legs crossed, body casual. I've seen this position a million times. At celebrations, at midnight meetings, at any event where he's speaking. Now he looks down at us, his blue eyes painted an unnaturally bright color blue.

I'm so caught up on this painting—disturbed by it, I don't even notice that at the foot of the bed, a circle has been drawn and single candle, surrounded by various stones, marks the middle.

Margaret looks up at the painting and says, "A reminder that this ceremony is blessed by Anex and all he wants is for you to find your true self." She squeezes my shoulder and moves to stands over the circle. "This is the circle of confession. A place where you will release the burdens that hold you back from your true self."

"Isn't that what Correction is about?"

She smiles, her lips looking elongated in the shadowy light. "This is different. It's about sharing your burdens to another woman. Someone who can help carry the weight." Her hands thrust over the circle and reach for mine. "It will be a journey; one we will take together. Are you ready?"

My heart thuds, a month ago this would have been a dream. Spending time with Anex's spiritual wife, would have fulfilled all of my wishes, but now... it's not just scary, it's terrifying. I have secrets. Big ones, ones that could hurt so many people.

But she doesn't wait for my response, stepping into the circle and drawing me in with her. We both sit, her on one side and me on the other. With my hands still in hers, and our knees parallel. Her smile is kind, and I remember who I am, how I was raised and what I believe.

The Way will always carry me through. Margaret is just another guide.

"I'm ready," I say, a few minutes too late.

"Good. Did you prepare like you were told?"

The folded-up paper burns in my pocket. I retrieve it, but don't hand it over. Not yet.

"Is that your collateral?" she asks.

"Yes," I say, my stomach rolling with uneasiness. "I wasn't exactly sure what you wanted."

Although, that's not entirely true. They want secrets. Dirt. Skeletons in the closet. The directions were clear, I was to write down a confession about something in my life, a secret no one else knew about, that if I told anyone about the woman's group or ever betrayed anyone else involved, that secret, or collateral, would be used against me.

For me, it wasn't a matter of if I had a secret that could be used for collateral, but which one I should share.

I'd thought hard about it. Channeled The Way. Searched for the right answer. There wasn't one. I could just as easily write down that Rex wants to destroy his father, that our Ordering is a sham, or that he's searching for the truth about my mother and his. I could tell them about the intensity of my Corrections: how it's moved beyond seeking Enlightenment for my Lapses and down a dark, seductive, rabbit hole I can't escape. I could confess to the panties in my drawer, the porn on Silas' computer... there are too many infractions to count.

But most of those were approved of by Anex. And the stuff about Rex? That's a betrayal with deep consequences. So, I wrote down the only thing that felt like it was big enough, but also everyone involved knew about.

"Just read me what you wrote down," Margaret says.

My hands shake, making the paper tremble. I look up at her and she nods. "Since my Ordering, I've been intimate with other men than Rex. A man of his stature has particular needs and wants. I was instructed to receive training from Rex's friends, preparing me for my future mate's unconventional needs and desires."

As I say the words, I'm sure that Margaret already knows this. She's been mentoring me for a while and is wise and Anex's closest confidant. But still, admitting it out loud, feels wrong and shameful.

"Did you enjoy this intimacy?" she asks.

"Sometimes," I confess. "They're difficult men. Not always nice. Demanding but..."

"But what?"

"But they know women and their bodies. They know what Rex wants in a mate and that is always my priority."

Margaret squeezes my hand and takes the paper from me. "You're a strong woman, Imogene."

"I don't feel strong." God, that's the most honest thing I've said in days. "I feel weak and lost and confused. I'm overrun with emotions and desires. It's like I'm a slave to my body, to these feelings I've never experienced before."

"You are doing the work of Serendee," Margaret says, "following

The Way. If Anex wants you to explore your sexuality with other men, then what you're doing must be right."

Because Anex is never wrong.

I take a deep breath. "Was that enough? Collateral?"

"More than enough," she says, leaning across the candle and tucking my hair behind my ear. "You've unloaded your burden, and I'm here to carry the weight. Are you sure there's nothing else?"

Loads, I almost say, but I just shake my head.

"And you don't think I'm a bad person for what I just told you?"

"Imogene, you're a beautiful, sexy woman. I know you were taught modesty and faithfulness to the man you were Ordered with, but not everyone is meant to follow the same path. You're part of the Chosen, mated with a powerful man, and that means different demands will be placed on you. We've talked about this before."

I know her relationship with Anex is different. He has many spiritual wives, but he's also special. I'm not special. I was chosen because Rex needed something from me, something I didn't fully understand until he asked me to contact my mother.

"Thank you for sharing this burden," I say, feeling the slightest weight off my shoulders. "Rex is torn between two worlds, and I'm determined to be the anchor that ties him to Serendee. I'll do anything for him."

I realize as soon as I say it that, the words are not only true, but they're the kind that get a person in trouble. I search Margaret's expression, but I don't see anything that implies she noticed. The unease doesn't subside as my mentor chants a mantra of healing and then extinguishes the candle. The hairs on the back of my neck stand on end as I pass Rex's childhood bedroom and descend the stairs.

It's not until I'm outside that I take a breath.

I *will* do anything for this man, which is startling and concerning. My duty as a member of Serendee isn't to devote myself to my mate.

It's to devote myself to our leader, his father.

14

E^{lon}

She doesn't notice me as she walks down the steps of the bungalow and up the road. Imogene is lost in a world of her own, and I can't help but wonder what transpires between her and the other women in the group. Knowing Anex, it's transactional and involves secrets, lies and manipulation. Other than money, those are the currencies he trades in.

I follow her, keeping an eye on her as she walks in the dark. Her blonde braid swings across her back. Unlike the women in the secular world, she's fearless. Those other women have a wariness about them. They've been conditioned to keep an eye over their shoulder, to be aware that bad men are out there. Men that hurt.

Imogene? Well, she's been conditioned to think that bad men are good. That hurt is love and that pain means you're following The Way.

It's not just her poor little brain that's fucked up. It's her body, too. I've never seen a woman crave hurt so much.

As she walks down our street, my phone vibrates in my pocket. I pull it out and look at the message.

Silas: Can you grab my kit.

Elon: Yes. What's up?

Silas: Meet me at the Main House. I'll explain then.

I hadn't planned on approaching her, but now that Silas needs his kit, I catch up as she opens the front door.

"Hold the door," I say, announcing myself. She turns at the sound of my feet pounding on the porch steps.

"Oh, sure," she says, cheeks flushing slightly. "I was just—"

"I need to grab something for Silas," I say, cutting her off before she is forced to tell a lie about where she's been. A lie that'll send her back down to that dungeon with Levi for Corrections. I step in the house and search the cubbies by the door. "Ah, there." I spot the blue case on the top shelf and pull it down. "Silas asked me to bring it to him."

"His First-Aid kit?" she asks, frowning. "Is he hurt?"

"No, I don't think so." I curl the handle in my fingers. "He said to bring it to the Main House."

"Someone is hurt," she says, eyes narrowing as she tries to piece it together. "Someone that can't see a healer?"

I hadn't even thought about it. Silas' job... it's not something I ask about. The things he is asked to do, the tasks Anex makes him perform... I'd rather not know.

Imogene and I share a look and I realize she understands this as well. She should. He's healed her wounds more than once. "I'm coming with you," she says suddenly.

I laugh. "No, you're not."

"Why?"

"Because Silas didn't call you."

"Call me? I don't have a phone, Elon. No one in this community has a phone but the four of you."

True. "I don't know what we're getting into, Little Lamb, and the farther you stay from the Main House, the better. Rex wouldn't want you up there."

"Well, Rex isn't home, and since when are you afraid to show me the under belly of Serendee?" Her arms cross under her breasts, drawing my eyes down. When I drag them back up her expression has softened, her eyes pleading. "Let me help."

It's then that I realize I can't tell this woman no. Not when she looks at me with those clear blue eyes and pink pouty lips. I run my hand through my hair and grunt, "Fine, but you stick by my side. No wandering off and if anything out of control happens, you get the fuck out of there, understood?"

"What could—" she starts to question, but I shoot her a look and she amends, "understood."

Silas waits for us by the backdoor, forehead creasing when he sees Imogene. His eyes dart to mine. "What is she doing here?"

"I wanted to come," she says, answering for herself. I shrug and hand him his kit.

I can tell he wants to argue, but there's also a current of urgency vibrating off of him. He just jerks his head toward the door and punches in the code to disable the lock. Once we're inside he takes a staircase that leads downstairs, then continues down a long hallway.

"What is this?" Imogene asks. I'm not sure myself, but a bad feeling inches up my spine. Silas has told us about The Fallen and how they live separately, in small rooms under the mansion. I'd never had an opportunity to see it for myself. No, I'd never wanted the opportunity. Sometimes it's better to live in the dark.

"I heard from one of the girls that Charlotte is struggling."

"Charlotte?" I vaguely recall the name.

"She's the girl Anex reprimanded the day we went shopping," Imogene says. "Anex punished her."

The memory clicks. "For contacting her sister?"

"Yes." Her hand reaches out to Silas' and she links their fingers. "What's wrong with her?"

He stops at another door and uses another code to get past the lock. On the other side is a long hallway, rows of closed doors, each with locks, on both sides. A small window looks into each room.

"This is where he keeps them." Silas says, walking past several doors. Imogene makes an effort to look inside, but I push her along. I'm not exactly sure what happens behind these doors, but I don't think it's anything she needs to see. "Charlotte was sent down here to consider her Lapses. Why she feels the need to reach outside of Serendee for affirmation from her family." Neither Imogene or I argue this, it's a standard rule of the community. No outsiders unless they're approved. "She's a strong female," Silas says, eyes sliding from Imogene to me. "But she wants to please Anex."

He enters the code, and the door opens. The sour scent of body odor greets us.

The room is tiny, barely big enough for a small, single, bed and a desk. Log books sit on the top, along with three pencils, all worn down to the nub. On the bed is a skinny girl. I barely recognize her from that day in Anex's room. Her hair is stringy. Her arms bone thin. Her skin pale and ashy.

Imogene sucks in a gasp, her fingers dropping from Silas' hand to move to her mouth.

"Hey," he says, getting her attention. She shifts her head slightly, eyes trying to focus.

"I filled out my logs. Every calorie. Every Lapse. Every negative thought." She moves to sit up, but she doesn't get far. It's obvious why. Her hand is cuffed to the bed.

"It's fine," Silas says, gesturing for her to lie back down. "I'm not here to check on your progress. I'm here to make sure you're okay."

"Is this a test?" she asks, eyes narrowing. "Are you here to test me? To make sure I'm worthy?"

"No. I know you're worthy." He runs his fingers over the purple bruises on her wrists.

"I'm not." It's almost a whisper. "I'm not worthy of Anex's grace. I broke the rules. I made this happen."

"Sweetheart, let me check you out. Can I do that?"

Her eyes slide from Silas to Imogene and then over to me. She visibly flinches when she sees me. "Are you going to tell?"

I blink. "Tell?"

"Anex. I know you're one of the Chosen. You're impossible to miss." She tries to sit up again but falls back. "Are you going to tell him about me?" Her voice trembles. "Tell him I won't cry. Not this time. I promise."

"No one is telling Anex anything," Imogene says, turns to me. "I think you should step outside."

"Excuse me?"

Silas looks over his shoulder. "She's right. Just stand outside the door. I think you make her uncomfortable."

"Why? I don't even know the girl."

"Elon," Imogene says, "this girl is hurt. She needs help, and you're very intimidating." My eyes skim over her again, noticing the purple bruises on her wrists. "Just wait outside. We can take care of this."

We?

Since when is she part of this? Any of this?

But I do step back, giving them some space. The room is small, and I'm a big man. Intimidating. I don't deny that. I watch as the two of them focus on her. Silas with his bag of first-aid ointments and salves he mixes himself. Small packets of medications he carries as part of his job. He's not a healer, not in the traditional sense, but he is a caregiver. One that specializes in the broken females of Serendee.

"Charlotte," Silas says, sitting on the edge of the bed. "I know this is uncomfortable, but I'm going to examine you. Make sure you're okay."

There is no world in which this girl is okay. Imogene picks up one of the logs on the table. Her finger runs down the pencil marks. "This is all you're eating?" she asks.

"They bring me food. I only eat half. I'm not Indulgent." Imogene's eyes flick to mine. Worried. "He likes me this way. The less I eat, the more he comes to... visit."

"He...?" Imogene asks.

"Anex."

While Imogene keeps her talking, Silas checks her skin for bruises, his fingers lingering over her inner thighs. From the door I see the purpling flesh—the imprint of a thumbprint. Charlotte pulls down her shirt, trying to cover them.

"How often does he come?" Silas asks, removing a protein bar from the kit and opening it. She stares at it like it's poison but he doesn't relent until she takes a bite.

"If I'm good he blesses me with multiple visits and oversees my re-education himself. Sometimes it's just once a day. Unless I cry. Then he makes me go through Corrections before he comes back." She gives a wobbly smile. "I almost never cry anymore."

Imogene picks up the second log and studies it. She moves closer to me, and I realize she's showing me the book—a calendar. Each day is filled with a series of X's. "Charlotte," she says, stepping toward the girl. "What do those marks mean?"

Her pale cheeks turn red, but her eyes shine with a dark glint. "That's when he comes. When he blesses me. I mark each time so I don't forget. Sometimes the days get confusing in here."

"He blesses you?" Imogene repeats. "Re-educates?"

"It's how I regain my status. Only Anex can work me though the levels of re-education." I didn't know for sure what Anex did with the Fallen. I didn't really care but seeing this girl—seeing Imogene's reaction to her—it stirs something in my chest. Charlotte looks up at her. "You're part of his family, aren't you? His son's mate." Imogene nods. "Will you tell him I won't be a bad girl anymore? I won't call my family. I can get the money. I'm here for him, always. I'm devoted."

Clutching the calendar against her chest, Imogene nods and turns abruptly, pushing past me to exit the room. Silas and I share a look and I follow her out. In the hall she's frantically peering into each window. I grab her. "Hey, I need you to settle down."

"Settle down?" she shouts. I drag her down the hall to the door and push her outside of the wing. The door slams behind us. "You want me to settle down after I saw that?"

"It was a lot," I admit, cupping the back of my neck. "What's happening down there—"

"He threatened to send me there," she says, cutting me off. "He said if my Bonding with Rex isn't real, he'll send me down with the Fallen, in the 'room I saved for your mother.'"

"Jesus," I mutter. "He's not going to do that."

"How do you know?" Her eyes are wild, full of uncertainty.

I grab her and pull her to me. "I know because he has to get through me to do that. He has to get through Silas and Levi and most of all Rex, who is more than willing to have an excuse to kill his father."

"Those 'blessings?' That's just him having sex with her, Elon," she says, as if I hadn't just spoken. She thrusts the calendar at me. "Multiple times a day all under the guise of 're-education.' All under the concept of being 'Better.'" Her voice rises. "He locks her up and uses her for his personal needs all day and night. Did you know about this?"

"This?" I ask, looking at the calendar—at the dark pencil marks documenting each and every time. "No. No more than you did."

"What does that mean?"

"It means, Anex uses the people of Serendee, Imogene. You know that. You've experienced it first-hand. You were raised in it just like the rest of us. We are at his mercy," I tell her. "He is our path to Enlightenment, isn't that how it goes?"

"What do you believe, Elon?" she asks. The tremble in her voice implies she knows how risky that question is. I answer it anyway.

"I don't know how I feel," I admit. "I'm caught somewhere between Rex and Levi. I know there is a bigger world out there, but unlike Rex, I don't believe I deserve it. I'm in Serendee because this is where I belong. I work for Anex because he is better than I am. If

I deserved more, I would be given more. Until then, I have a job, and I'm thankful for that."

"And what exactly is that job?" she asks.

"Right now, it's training you to be a better mate for my best friend." I swallow, knowing it goes deeper than that. The secrets and lies. "Tomorrow it may be something different, but until I'm given different orders, my job is protecting the future of Serendee."

"And if that means leaving that girl in there to be," she swallows, "'blessed' by Anex every day for the rest of her life, then you'll do it."

I will. She knows it and so do I, but there's something else she's not admitting.

She doesn't have what it takes to save that girl either.

15

───────

I mogene

When we return home, Rex and Levi are waiting.

"Where have you been?" Rex asks, eyes darting between me and Elon. Neither of us spoke on the way back to the house. The disgust and guilt over what I'd witnessed is too much to bear.

"Silas needed help," Elon says. "I took Imogene with me rather than her be here all alone."

"Anex has called a late-night basketball game for the men," Levi says, "Mandatory."

"Son of a—" Elon mutters. "Tell him I'm sick. Or running a job. I'm not in the mood."

"Who is?" Rex says. "You're going. I can't afford having him look into any of our activities right now."

Elon glances at me, jaw hard. Rex is right. Anex doesn't need to ask questions about where I'd been earlier, at the women's meeting, or then up at the house. It puts us all at risk for being defiant.

"Fine." He walks over to the refrigerator and opens the cabinet above. He pulls out a bottle of clear liquor, unscrews the cap and takes a swig. "But if I'm going, I'm going drunk."

Levi grabs his notebooks and shakes his head. He stops by me and says quietly, "Everything okay?"

"Just tired that's all." I give him a tight grin. "It was a busy day."

"Get some rest." He runs his fingers gently down my neck. "When Anex calls the men like this, it's viewed as a moment of respite for the women. Take the opportunity to recharge and reflect."

The last thing I want to do is reflect on what I saw up in the Main House.

"I will," I say, watching him step out the door. Elon follows with his bottle of liquor, barely looking me in the eye. Rex follows, but I grab his wrist and tug him back. His eyebrow raises.

"I spent some time today looking for answers to your question."

"Any luck?"

I shake my head. "Not yet, but I'll keep trying."

"Thank you," he says, resting his large hand on my hip, thumb rubbing tiny circles. "I guess you get a night off from our arrangement."

"Levi said it was an opportunity to recharge and reflect."

He snorts. "Like my father gives anyone a night off from anything."

"Try not to get in a fist fight with your father, okay?"

"Is that a request?"

"I just..." I think about Charlotte, her broken mind and body. Rex is the only thing keeping me out of a room like that. "I just want you to remember that you have a bigger plan."

His crystal blue eyes hold mine, and I have no idea what this man is thinking. But his hand rises to my chin, and he tilts my mouth towards his and he kisses me. For once it's not forceful, but his jaw is strong, tongue sweeping against mine. I feel the rush of our connectivity surge through me. Me and Rex... we've had this chemistry from the start, all the way back to that day we stumbled onto one another at the overlook when we were kids, bonded by our mothers.

Here we are again, literally 'bonded' by that and more.

"Good night, Imogene," he says, after he pulls away. My lips feel hot as does my skin, warming me after such a traumatizing night.

I'm still processing it, when Silas comes in, worn and exhausted looking. He returns his kit to the cubby by the door and barely looks up when I enter the foyer.

"Hey, can I get you something to eat? Drink?"

He shakes his head and walks past me, going to his room. A moment later I hear the water running in the shower. I stand in the doorway, caught in confusion. Should I do something? When I learned about caring for the man in my life, it centered around food and keeping the house orderly. Silas taught me more about how to make a man feel good, but that doesn't seem right, not now. He's also not my man.

I tap my fingers on my thigh. Or is he? Aren't they all? Isn't that what Rex told me he wanted? A woman for his friends who Anex would never give one of their own.

The urge to comfort Silas, the way he has comforted and soothed me through my own pain overwhelms me and without hesitation I stride into his room and enter the bathroom. The glass is fogged from the steam, but I see the shadowy outline of his naked body behind it. I peel off my dress, goosebumps rising on my flesh from the cool air, and open the shower door. Silas has his face lifted to the running shower, as if he's trying to wash away everything he'd seen, but he turns when he hears the door open.

"Hey," I say, sliding in the shower behind him. He doesn't move, and I wrap my arms around his waist, leaning into him. "Do you want to talk about it? We don't have to. I just..." I press my cheek against his warm, strong, back, "I didn't know you had to do things like that."

He reaches for my hand and pulls it tight against his toned belly. "I don't, and Anex will be pissed to find out I interfered, but I feel an obligation to these women."

I hear his heartbeat under my ear and feel his muscles tense at my touch. He's a strong man but filled with emotion and compassion. So different from the other guys.

"You aren't the one that hurt her, Silas. Anex did that."

He turns to face me. Our belly's touching. His cock half-erect and pressing between my thighs. "I played my part. Rex gets them in the door, Levi into classes and I... well, I strip away their inhibition. I confuse their mind and their bodies. I show them what feels good, so that they forget the bad." His forehead drops to my shoulder. "I own my guilt in this, Imogene. The least I can do is try to relieve a little of the pain."

I force his head up until I can see his face. "Did you give her the comfort she needed?"

"I gave her some medication." His mouth forms a frown. "She has an infection—from too much sex and inappropriate hygiene."

"Why would he allow that?" I ask, so confused by the actions of our leader.

"Because he can?" Hot water runs between us, but he shivers anyway, and I press my chest to his, trying to give him warmth. "He takes, Little Lamb, and when he notices you enough to give you something in return, it's never good."

His words hit my heart like a hammer, and the smallest piece chips away. I don't know what it means, or what any of us can do, but I have to act in some way. I look up at this man, so handsome and kind, so talented and skilled. I grab the soap and lather it in my hands, then gently scrub his skin.

He watches me as I work, coating his shoulders and then down to his chest, my fingers gliding down his hard flesh. His muscles tense, and his abdomen caves, quivering under my touch. His hands reach out for me, fingering my nipple, and watching it rise to a hard peak.

"You don't need to—" I start, wanting to focus on him, make him feel better, but he cups my breasts in his large hands and pushes them together, then drops his mouth to latch on.

The sensation runs through me, electric shocks that run

straight between my legs. He moves to the other breast, and licks and sucks just as greedily, eliciting a moan that echoes off the bathroom tiles.

Silas looks up at me, eyes dark with heat. His mouth crashes against mine, kissing me with intensity. I've never felt him like this —so raw and feral. I didn't know he had this side to him. I hold onto him tight, wanting him to pour all of that into me.

I shift backwards, searching for the wall. I find it and drag him to me, hiking a leg over his hip, feeling his length between my thighs.

"Fuck me," I tell him, finding the words he taught me. "Fuck me and make this all go away."

His eyes meet mine and a dark glint shines back. "You're just another one of my sins, Imogene. Another victim to add to the list."

"No," I tell him. "I'm not one of your victims. I'm one of *you*. One of us. Born and raised for this moment."

His hands move under me, lifting me off the floor. My back is pressed against the tile and the tip of his cock probes urgently at my entrance. I rock my hips, desperate to feel him inside of me. Somehow, he holds back. "You don't belong to me, Imogene."

"Is that what you think?"

"It's what I know. Anex wants me for his own use. He'll never give me an Order."

"Fuck his Orders, Silas." I kiss away the shock of my Regression, licking his lips, his tongue. "Rex owns me, and he has opened our life to you. All of you. He loves you that much and I—" I swallow the word. Love is complicated in Serendee. I rock my hips against him again and this time his cock inches in, stretching me slowly. "This is between us, the five of us, not *him*." I bite down on my bottom lip and then whisper, "Don't make me beg, not tonight."

Something in him breaks, like a dam crumbling under the pressure. His hips rear back, and he eases in, filling me with his length. The air knocks out of me, and he does it again, with deep sweeping thrusts. Even in all of this, Silas is a man of skills, a man that knows how to make a woman feel good. My tits bounce against his chest, grazing my nipples over the hard muscles, sending shockwaves through my nerves. He spreads my ass cheeks, and massages in the spot he'd explored before, eliciting shuddering quivers from back to front. He isn't hard and fast, or lost to his own demons like Rex. He doesn't pound into me like Rex, trying to bruise every inch of my soul. With Silas, every movement is intentional, delicious, and by the time the orgasm rolls over me, my entire body begs for release.

"Keep doing that," I cry, and he captures my mouth once again. I taste his tongue, swallow his hot breath, as the orgasm comes hard, a bright blinding light, in a sea of darkness. Silas doesn't stop until his body tenses, muscles undulating, hips rocking, until his seed fills me—our bodies tight and loose at the same time.

His mouth releases me at the same time he unsheathes himself, gently lowering me back to the floor. He takes the next few minutes to clean me up, washing away his cum with the cooling water.

Wrapped in warm towels, we stand just outside the shower, soaking the floor mat beneath our feet.

"Thank you," he says, pushing the wet hair off my shoulder. "No one's ever done that for me before."

I frown. "Done what?"

What he says next doesn't just break my heart, it shatters my soul. "Take care of me like that."

"Because you're always taking care of everyone else?" I ask, trying to understand. Silas has a position of authority in Serendee. He's chosen, but tonight showed me he's responsible for the most bruised and broken of us all. "It doesn't have to be that way. I'm here for you. The guys are here for you. We can shoulder some of the burden."

"No," he says, voice firm. "It's my place. Not yours. My duty to Serendee."

I blink, the truth of it all crashing down. "This is wrong, Silas. This is not what The Way is about. Our bodies are temples. We keep them clean and pure so we can become Enlightened."

He laughs, it's dark and lacking humor. "No number of lectures,

Corrections or showers will make me clean enough for Enlightenment, Imogene."

I grab his hand, still damp. "What do you mean? Everyone can earn their way back. Even the Fallen."

"I wish that were true," he says. "I mean, I wish I could believe it. I used to, during those early days, when I was being trained. I thought I was working toward the greater good, that I was blessed with this face and this body, my persuasive nature by The Way, to help build Serendee into a place of wonder." His fingers thread through mine. "But now I'm not so sure." He drops his forehead to mine. "I just feel so dirty. No matter how many showers I take."

"But—"

He kisses me gently. "Thank you. For being you and giving me this moment."

With a squeeze of my hand he exits the bathroom. I'm struck by the simplicity of what he said, how even though this man is one of the Chosen and integral to the stability and growth of Serendee, he is just as lost as the rest of us. Rex may be right. I may need to be the anchor for all of these men. The question is will they let me?

16

————

I mogene

I STARE at the dinner on the table... baked chicken, roasted vegetables, fresh from the Serendee garden, and mashed potatoes. A bowl of fruit and a homemade pie sit on the counter. All of it is cold now , having come out of the oven hours ago.

I look at my watch. Eleven PM.

Not one of them told me they wouldn't be here. And one in particular promised he'd come home at night. I guess that lasted all of two days.

I didn't just cook. I changed after work into one of the outfits Elon picked out for me, trying to be obedient to my mate's desires when he got home.

I'm *trying,* but I don't see how this works if he doesn't hold up to his end of the deal.

Twenty more minutes go by when I hear the front door open.

Levi steps in eyes darting from the table full of food to me, sitting alone.

"Hey," he says, shrugging off his coat. "This looks amazing."

"It's cold," I announce. "I thought you'd all be home hours ago."

"Oh." He frowns and pushes his fiery red hair out of his eyes. "I had a late class at the Center, and Elon got called in to make a delivery." He picks a blueberry out of the bowl. "Silas went with him."

My jaw tightens and I will myself not to ask, "And Rex?" but it comes out anyway, bitter and harsh.

"I, uh," his hand swipes through his hair again, "I think he had some business to attend to on campus."

My eyebrow raises. "Business?"

"At the fraternity house," he admits. "It's good for him to be seen while his product is in use and, well, a good place to recruit."

"Women."

"Mostly, yes." His head tilts. "Are you questioning his service to Serendee?"

I snort. "He's at a party, Levi, not conducting a business meeting, and I'm aware of how Rex 'recruits' women. Will he sweet talk them back? Who does he hand them over to next? You or Silas?"

His forehead creases and he crosses over to me. "What's this about?"

Shame fills me. I'm being Indulgent, thinking only of myself and my desires. I drop my eyes from Levi's gaze. "Nothing. I just went to all this trouble to make dinner, and it would be nice if someone had told me none of you were going to be here."

"Well, I'm here now." He takes my hand and kisses the back of it. "Let me go shower and clean up. Then we can eat together."

I give him a tight smile and hold it until he's in his room, door shut behind him. All I can think of is Rex being at a party. Surrounded by secular women. I've witnessed this before, the way they hang on him in their tight clothes. He's handsome. Charismatic. He is his father's son after all.

Knowing he's out there, with them, creates a twist in my belly that is unfamiliar. An urge to find him and force him home. I stare at the food on the table and make a split moment decision.

I leave.

I can hear the sound of the shower running as I slip through the dark streets. I stick to the shadows, knowing that if I'm caught out late like this, alone, there will be consequences. Most of the other houses are dark. It's late. People work early and have long days. You never know when Anex will send out the signal and call us all to a lecture. The awareness of these facts only makes me angrier and more upset that Rex has pushed me to this point.

My hands tremble as I push open the gate, stepping over the line that divides Serendee from the Secular world, leaving the quiet behind. The world seems loud when I go outside the walls. Noisy and disruptive. There are so many people. So many eyes and cars and glowing devices. Sometimes the people barely notice me—so focused on their phones. But when they do it's like a wolf stumbling upon a single lamb... "Little Lamb," they call me. I understand it when I'm out here.

Tonight though, no one takes much notice. Not when I pass the bar or the late-night café. I realize it's because of my outfit. Jeans and a fitted shirt. A girl stares at me, and I realize it's the braid. I tug it out as I walk, letting it fall over my shoulders in waves.

I head toward campus, walking quickly past The Center on the way. I know where the fraternity row is located and I turn down the path that leads toward the street made of big blocky houses. These buildings make sense to me. A group of young people all sharing a home? A domum? I've lived this life—just in another world.

The party isn't hard to find. I just follow the people walking down the street. I watch them. Study the way the girls' hips move so easily, how the boys touch them without care. It's like the TV shows Silas had me watch. There's so much freedom here, while also, tension and stress.

I reach the house—three stories, red brick with columns. Greek letters hang over the door, Zeta Sigma. I'm shocked they don't fall off from the vibration of the music inside. From the sidewalk, I can feel it bouncing in my chest. People cluster on the porch. Men, women, dressed in a variety of ways. All clutching red cups in their grip.

Rex is inside there. I know it. Sense it, but another awareness comes slamming home; this is not my world. What was I thinking coming down here? I wasn't. I was being Indulgent. Lapsing. Everything I've strived not to be.

"I'm not sure what's going on in that pretty little head of yours, but it must be intense."

It takes me a moment to realize those words were meant for me.

"Excuse me?" I ask, taking a look at the man in front of me. He's tall. Lanky but broad. Shoulders wide and powerful. He's wearing a hoodie with a 'W' on the chest. An X underneath it made out of two oars. 'Wittmore Rowing' is embordered in white thread.

"You just look a little lost and confused, although I don't know why," he grins. "You're exactly the kind of girl we love to see at our parties." He offers me his hand. "I'm Knox."

I stare at his hand. I've never touched a man outside of Serendee. Never had a conversation this long. He tilts his head, line creasing his forehead and I snap out of it, thrusting my hand into his. "I'm Imogene. I'm uh, new here."

"Imogene." He rolls the word on his tongue. "Unique, but I like it." He looks over my shoulder. "Hey Miller," he calls. I turn and see another man. This one is also tall, blue-eyed with a devilish-purely Indulgent glint in his eye. "Meet Imogene. She's new."

His smirk spreads into a wide grin. "Well, then, we need to give Imogene the Zeta Sigma new student treatment, don't you think?"

Knox nods, winking over my head. He throws his arm over my shoulder, and the two of them usher me past the guy standing at the door, through a crowd of mostly women, toward the kitchen. I search the house for Rex, but it's too thick with students and an ever-present cloud of smoke, that I don't see him. Maybe he's not even here? Miller grabs me one of the red cups and hands it to me.

"Welcome to Wittmore and Zeta Sig." Miller holds his own cup to mine, except his is black, not red. "May tonight be a night you won't soon forget."

I sniff the drink. It smells fruity, not sour like the heavy wine Elon forced me to drink a few weeks ago. I'm trying to think of a nice way to decline, when I spot a familiar blond head across the room. His jawline is unmistakable, as is his smile.

I rarely see it, but he's not holding back here, gracing some girl in short shorts and a tank top with its full intensity. Jealousy, dark and angry flares in the pit of my stomach and I tip the cup to my lips and swallow. The sweetness is followed by a burn. I cough and feel a warm hand on my shoulder.

"You okay?"

"I'm fine." I smile and take another, smaller sip. "Thank you."

"No, sweetheart," Miller says, "thank you for gracing us with your beauty tonight. We like to have the most beautiful girls on campus at our party. You just notched it up to a ten."

After weeks of battling the men in my life, of living on the edge of pain and humiliation, Corrections and Lapses and Regression, his words untangle something in my chest. Just hearing kind words, not laced inside twisted manipulations... I feel a rush of relief.

"Drink up," Knox says, "and let us show you a good time and forget about whatever put that frown on your face."

"Okay," I say, eyeing Rex and his plaything across the room. "Yes. Please show me a good time."

His fingers link with mine, warm and firm. Miller's hand lands on my lower back, guiding me to follow. Soon we're in the middle of the room, dancing in a throng of people. The music is loud, my blood hums. It's weird and wild and kind of reminds me of the late night celebrations back at Serendee, except here there's no watchful eye following and judging our moves. No Anex pulling the strings.

"God you're beautiful," Knox says, running his fingers through my hair.

"You're pretty, too," I say back. The room grows a little fuzzy. I laugh and both boys laugh with me. I lift my cup and take another sip of my drink. Someone bumps into me and the liquid sloshes, sending a wave cascading down my chin.

"Oh," I say, trying to catch it. Miller steps forward and lifts the hem of his shirt, using it to wipe off the mess. I eye his abdomen, ripped with a ladder of hard muscle. "Thank you."

"Come on," he says, taking my hand. "Let's go clean you up."

Again, I'm led through the party, passing people that no longer take full shape. Miller pulls me into a room. It's a pantry of sorts, with a counter and small sink. He shuts the door behind us and turns on the faucet, then grabs a cloth out of a cabinet. He wets the cloth and wipes my chin and neck, smiling as he does it. I sigh and lean against the counter. "That feels good," I say, as he gently wipes my chest. "It was hot in there."

"No baby, that's all you." His fingers graze my neck. "Smokin'. I can't believe you just wandered in here off the street. Like a goddamn vision." I reach for the cup to take another sip. He grabs it from me and sets it on the counter. "You may want to slow down on that."

I look up at his chiseled jaw and say, "I wish I grew up in a world like this, with boys like you."

His forehead creases. "What kind of boy am I?"

"Sweet," she says, "Nice."

He chuckles and pushes the hair off my neck. "Exactly what world did you grow up in?"

"Serendee," I say, the word sliding off my tongue. "I'm from Serendee."

He pulls back. "The cult?"

"It's not a cult," I respond. My fingers feel weird. Numb. "It's utopia."

He shrugs. "I knew you were different. Special." His hand slips under the hem of my shirt. "I've heard about you girls. You look all innocent and sweet, but it's really all about sex, right?"

The statement echoes in my head. I've heard something like it before—out on the street when I was accosted by men before my Ordering. Rex, Elon, Silas and Levi protected me. At the time I thought the accusations were gross. Completely off base, but maybe... god, maybe they aren't. Sex has become the focus of my life.

I open my mouth to respond but the door swings open behind Miller. He's yanked back by his collar.

"Get your fucking hands off my woman." Rex looms in the doorway, a murderous glint in his eye. He tosses Miller into the hallway, back slamming against the wall.

"Hey, man, I didn't do anything to her. She spilled her drink, and I just helped her clean up."

"Bullshit. I saw you out on the dance floor, pawing at her like an animal." He steps forward and grabs him by the front of his shirt. Miller isn't small, but Rex? He's honed and sharp. I realize it now; deadly.

My heart pounds, and I curl against the counter terrified of what Rex will do. We don't abide by secular laws in Serendee. Touching another man's mate? Rex could skin him alive and Anex would give him the blade, but even I know the rules are different here.

"Stop!" I shout, lunging at Rex. I grab his bicep, tense and bulging. "Don't."

"Not now, Imogene." He attempts to shrug me off, but I hold on with both hands. "I don't know what the fuck you're doing here, but no one touches you without my permission." His hand balls into a fist. "Not even this pretty, entitled frat boy."

"Woah," a voice says from the hall. Knox appears, holding his hands up. "What's going on."

"Your *brother* brought my woman back here."

He looks around Rex and spots me. He's quiet for a moment then says, "Imogene, right?"

"Yes."

"Yeah, she told us she came here looking for you, didn't you?"

I don't know who this guy is, or what kind of game he's playing, or how he knew, but we're not in Serendee. There are laws out here and Rex can't just beat a man to death because he took me in a pantry. Especially since I went willingly. "Yes," I say. "I came here for you."

His shoulders relax minimally and he looks down. "Why?"

"You didn't come home like you promised."

He stares at me long and hard then turns back to Miller. He tightens his grip on his shirt, cutting off his air, before shoving him back, "Get the fuck out of my face and stay the hell away from women that don't belong to you."

"Dude," Miller says, rubbing his neck and inching down the hall, "you're in *our* house."

"Yeah, and everyone in this place is high on the weed I supplied." Rex shrugs. "I can take my business elsewhere."

Knox grabs Miller by the shoulder and pulls him down the hallway. "Just leave it dude. Royer's gonna kick your ass when he finds out about all this."

"Shut up," he says, shrugging Knox away. He starts down the hall and turns back and gives me a wink. "Just a tip, you've got about another thirty minutes with her before she's completely incoherent."

A growl rips through Rex's chest, but instead of going after Miller he pushes me back inside the pantry and slams the door shut. His eyes dart to the cup. "You drank from that?"

"It's just a punch," I tell him.

"Yeah, made with a hundred proof and laced with GHB."

I don't know what either of those things are. He lifts me off the floor and sets me on the counter, grabbing my chin and tilts my face upward, thumbing under my eyes and peering into each one. "What are you doing?"

"How much did you have?"

"Not that much," I say. He continues to inspect me, fingers sliding down my throat and stopping over my pulse. "A couple sips. It burned my throat and I spilled half of it." I look toward the door. "Miller actually made me stop drinking it."

"Yeah, he probably wanted you coherent when he fucked you."

My jaw drops. "He wasn't going to—"

"Yeah, Little Lamb, that's exactly what he planned to do." His fingers drop from my neck, down my arm. "You walked right into the slaughterhouse; you know that? And for what? To drag me home?"

"You promised." I have nowhere to put my hands, and my brain is a little fuzzy, so I rest them on his stomach. His muscles tense. "You said you'd come home, every night."

"This is work."

I roll my eyes. "That girl you were talking to was work?"

"Recruitment," he says simply. "I have a quota. You know that, Imogene."

I do, but it doesn't lessen the sting. "You defy your father all the time, but not when it comes to other women. That's about you, not him."

"That's about me doing what I'm told so that he doesn't get suspicious and start sniffing around more than he already is." He tilts his head. "Did anyone see you leave?"

"No. Elon and Silas are doing a job. Levi was in the shower."

He snorts. "He's probably panicking right now."

"Probably," I say feeling a little guilty.

"You can't walk the streets alone, Imogene."

"I was dressed like a secular girl. No one noticed me."

"Oh, they noticed you," he says, running his finger over the collar of my shirt. "Those two assholes were on you the second they saw you."

"They were just—"

"Men." He pushes his fingers under my shirt. "Men are aware of you, Little Lamb. They see your beauty. Smell your innocence. They want to be the ones to break you in, claim a little piece of you."

"That's not true," I say, squirming against his touch. My skin warms and my nipples tighten. He notices and brushes the pad of his thumb over the peak. I suck in a breath and shiver. "I just looked lost, and they were being—"

"Don't you fucking dare say nice." I swallow back the excuse and lean into him. "If another man touched you—violated you—without my permission, I'd have to kill him."

"You wouldn't."

He shoots me a look, one that tells me I don't understand the lengths he'd go to protect his possessions. "You're mine, Imogene, inside the walls of Serendee *and* out. No one has the right to touch you, speak to you or be near you without my consent."

"You don't believe in the rules of The Way," I say, pretending his words don't send a pool of heat between my legs.

"I don't," he agrees, leaning forward and running his nose along the shell of my ear. "This has nothing to do with Serendee, and everything to do with you and me."

His lips capture mine, not gentle. Not demanding. Owning. He kisses me. Hard. Jaw working against mine at the same time his fingers push up my shirt and his hands massage my breasts.

He licks my chin, my neck and along the path where the liquor spilled earlier. He doesn't stop until he's removed my shirt and has my tits pressed together, mouth consuming both of my nipples at once. I slam my head back, knocking it against the cabinet, and he lifts me cleverly unbuttoning my jeans and dragging them over my hips.

He pulls back and looks at me, eyes grazing over my body, one hand shifting up and down the bulge in his pants. My soul sets on fire.

I wait for him to release himself, to free that weapon cloaked in cotton, but he gives it one last long stroke and focuses back on me. He kisses the inside of one knee, then the other, then spreads apart my shaking thighs. His lips are warm, but the kisses leave a wet patch that cools, sending shivers across my flesh.

"You don—"

"Yes, Imogene, I do."

His tongue swipes over the hot patch of skin and my hips rise. I grip his shoulders for stability. "Rex," I start, trying to maintain composure. He inhales my scent, then parts my folds, pushing his tongue inside. It's wet and warm and— "Yes. Oh—"

His tongue dips in and out, circling. I drop my hands to the counter, curling them over the edge, and snap my thighs shut, the sensation too much, too overwhelming—

"Don't come," he says. "Not yet."

"But—" isn't that the point? Isn't that why he's doing this? To show me how he can make me feel? How much control he has over me?

"Not yet. Hold onto it, Little Lamb." He lifts his eyes to meet mine. "Hold onto me."

I pry my fingers from the edge of the counter and skim them over those hard biceps, up to his shoulders. He dives back in, tongue working against my clit. I shut my eyes and dig my nails into his rock-hard shoulders.

"Jesus, you taste so fucking good."

That's what does it. That's what unbinds me from my body, unravels the tight coils in the pit of my stomach. I rise off the counter, and he grabs my ass with both hands, stuffing his face with my pussy. His movements are slow, dragging licks across my frayed nerves. It's good. It's amazing. It's too, *too* much. It's heat and fire and boiling liquid and— "Rex," I push against his forehead, unable to bear it anymore. "Please..."

I feel one last touch, one faint press, a kiss between my legs before he rises. I stare at him through glazed eyes, taking in his red mouth and flushed cheeks. He's always handsome, but right now he looks boyish, like he'd been caught stealing cake.

He shifts himself, grimacing, and I wait for him to take out his cock, to grab me, to pin me to the counter and fuck me hard.

He doesn't. He opens the cabinet next to my head and pulls out a clean cloth. How he knew they were there is beyond me, but he runs the cloth under the water and carefully cleans between my legs. Without another word, he helps me off the counter and back into my jeans.

"Are you not going to..." I start. He pauses, looking at me. "You know... fuck me?"

"Definitely," he says, lip quirking. "But not now. Not when

you're drugged," he says simply. "And not when I'm feeling," he pauses, "so territorial."

"But you just—" I shake my head. He's so confusing. He's never worried about consent before.

He rests a hand on my shoulder. "It won't happen again."

Wait, what? What won't happen again? Because that... I really want it to happen again. "Rex—"

"Staying out late." He interrupts me. "It won't happen again. I made a promise to you. I'll stick to it, but don't forget, you made one to me, too."

I do everything he says. *Everything.*

I nod, and he takes my hand, leading me out of the pantry, down the hall and out into the warm night. Rex has claimed me, inside and out of Serendee. Whatever arrangement we've made, I realize that reaches beyond the bond we made in front of his father and the community as a whole.

I have no idea what that means.

17

E lon

FACING THE MIRROR, I swipe the razor down my chin, removing the last strip of stubble. Twisting my neck, I check to make sure I got everything. I don't see anything I missed, but what I do see is how fucking tired I look.

Last night had been long.

Anex is determined to expand our territory—pushing for us to make contacts outside of Wittmore University and local buyers. No one inside Serendee knows it, but the rumors about what's going on behind our walls are starting to gain steam. The word cult is tossed around a lot, as well as scam, con-artist, and charlatan. None of these are good for business or recruitment.

I dry off, patting my face with a towel, then my chest where a few droplets landed during my shave. I unwrap the towel around my waist and hang it on the hook behind the bathroom door and replace it with black pants. In the bedroom, I open the closet and notice a shadow under the bedroom door. I pause, waiting to see if someone is going to knock, but nothing comes. The shadow doesn't move.

I stride over and open the door. Imogene is frozen in her spot, fist poised to knock. Her eyes stare straight ahead—at my chest, then travel downward. She swallows thickly.

"What?" I ask, pressing my hand to the doorjamb.

"Never mind," she says, turning to leave. I snatch her wrist before she's too far out of reach and yank her back.

"I don't have time for your dramatics today," I snap. "What do you want, Imogene?"

Her eyes drop to the ground. "I'm sure you're busy—I can ask Silas."

"You can ask me," I reply, not releasing her. Her arm is narrow as a reed down by the lake. "What do you want?"

"I need someone—you—to take me outside of Serendee."

I drop my hand and cross both arms over my chest. Her eyes lift, taking in my muscles and my dick twitches. I ignore it. "Take you where?"

"Well, that's the thing. I'm not exactly sure. It's for, um," she looks over her shoulder, although we're home alone, "for something Rex asked me to do. I don't exactly understand everything he told me to do, but I figured you would."

Why does hearing this make my stomach clench uncomfortably? She came to me because I'm the kind of guy that will break the rules of Serendee. The shade of gray in this otherwise black and white world. "What does he want?"

"I'd rather not talk about it here." Her hands twist in the fabric of her dress. "Can you take me into town?"

The answer should be no. The response should be for me to go straight to Anex and tell him that a member of his community is behaving with Regressive intent. But that isn't who I am, which is exactly why she came to me for help. "I'll do you one better. I've got business two towns over. Whatever you need to do, we can do it there—away from any potential complications."

Complications means, Anex or any of his people.

"Should I change?" she asks.

I look down at her pale blue dress and the little embroidered flowers. Growing up in Serendee, seeing the girls covered up and revered, gave me intense fantasies about what happened underneath the soft cotton. Then we started going outside of the community, finding women who dressed provocatively and were willing to let us do all the things we were told we couldn't do inside the walls. Indulgent things. Regressive acts because we were not waiting until Anex gave his Order. But these dresses, the thin cotton, and high collars, the godforsaken buttons. It never failed to make me hard, and those fantasies, they never went away, even after I'd had my fill of secular flesh and pussy. My cock tightens in my pants, desperate and ready to be unleashed. And the way Imogene looks at me, I know she wouldn't fight if I bent her over the nearest surface and claimed her like a beast.

Like I've done before.

I swallow all that back. Now isn't the time, and this isn't the girl that deserves such treatment. She's trying so hard to be good, to serve her mate, and she ought to have someone much worthier than a man like me.

"Yes," I say, looking away from her. "You should change in to something more secular. I'll meet you out front in ten minutes."

"Thank you, Elon. I really appreciate it."

I reply with a grunt and step back in my room. Ten minutes, I think, heading straight to the bathroom. I open the drawer under the sink and pull out a bottle of lube with one hand while unbuttoning my pants with the other. Ten minutes to get rid of this boner so I can spend the rest of the day without acting like a feral animal in heat.

I pour the lube in my hand and oil up my cock, making it good and slippery. With one hand on the counter and the other stripping my cock, I close my eyes, not wanting to see my face as I think of the way I'd defile my best friend's mate. I know he doesn't care, but I do. She's too good for me. Too pure, and the way I jerk myself off while thinking about her like this is further proof.

Stroke.

I'm disgusting.

Stroke.

A degenerate.

Stroke.

I'm a man unworthy of his own mate and Anex knows it.

Stroke.

Imogene is too good for me. Too Enlightened. Too—*I think of her, bent over, ass bloody from the strap, begging me to go harder—*

Groan

I lurch, fingers curling around the edge of the sink as cum spills into the basin. I milk my cock, pushing out every last drop and take a deep breath, hopeful, that this will make the trip with Imogene a little bit more bearable.

Hopeful, but not confident.

〜

"Wait," she says, looking at the ramshackle building on the side of the road. "Exactly what are we doing here?"

"Business," I reply, shifting over my jacket to check the gun I tucked into my pants. When I look over again her jaw is loose.

"This is where you have business?" she asks, looking at the organized piles of tomatoes and cucumbers. "I'm confused. We have our own produce. And why do you need a gun?"

I frown and glance out the window of the truck. I drove the F-450. Completely inappropriate for a road trip, but I like how powerful it feels in my hands. There's one customer picking through a stack of melons and it strikes me that bringing Imogene with me was a bad idea. The average female resident of Serendee has no idea about the collection of fire power Anex has accumulated in this armory. Imogene would know that there are guns for hunting and general security, but this goes beyond that. Me, Rex,

Levi, Silas and any other male in the inner circle have been trained extensively for a breach of the walls—to defend the property and our business.

"Elon, why do you need a gun?" she repeats.

I watch the customer reach for her wallet and scratch my forehead with my thumb. "Because I'm not here to buy organic fruit. I'm here to collect on an outstanding payment. It's a pretty standard situation, but since you're with me, I'm not taking any chances."

The customer finally leaves, and I exit the cab. Walking around the back to grab the basket of green beans I brought with us from the farm, I do a quick check for the two kilos of hard-packed marijuana underneath. With the basket in one hand, I wrench open Imogene's door and offer her my hand to get down. A warm buzz passes between us during the few seconds we touch. She's in a cute striped T-shirt and navy-blue shorts that reveal her long legs. Very college co-ed. Very innocent but sexy.

Fuck. Now is not the time to get hard.

Walking into the open-air stand, I move slightly in front of Imogene. It smells of hay and fresh food, dirt and greenery. A man in overalls and a wide brimmed hat arranges husks of corn in a large pile, while a female in a heavy jumper and bonnet cuts up a cantaloupe by the counter. Soft strains of guitar music waft through the breezy shed.

"Morning, Jeb," I say, eyes combing the area for anything out of place. Everything is quiet, quaint and normal. Well, as normal as can be.

"Elon," he says with a nod, eyes flicking to Imogene. "Wasn't expecting you today."

"Well, I had some extra time, and it turns out you and I have some unfinished business."

Jeb's eyebrow arches. He plays like he's a small-town, innocent farmer, and not a shrewd businessman. He and Anex are cut from the same cloth. It's not a surprise that they found one another, or that one is trying to get one over the other.

"Honey, offer this young woman a piece of that cantaloupe,

while the men handle our affairs," he says, smiling over at Imogene. "So sweet you wouldn't believe it."

Imogene looks to me for approval. I nod, keeping an eye on her.

"Thought your women dressed more modestly in Serendee."

"Who said she was from Serendee?" I say, not liking the way he's looking at her.

He grunts and darkness flickers in his eye. I should've made her wear her normal clothes. Why did I bring her? Deep in my chest the truth threatens to reveal itself. My Indulgency will be my undoing. My desire to see her skin, to have her close, to pretend like she could be mine.

I follow him behind a sheet of burlap that acts as a barrier between the 'shop' and the back. Keeping an eye on Imogene through the sliver of space, I say, "It's my understanding that my runners shorted you last time. I apologize" I hold up the basket. "Two kilos of our best batch."

He takes the basket and pushes aside the beans, finding the drugs underneath. He must like what he sees, because he reaches behind his bib overall and pulls out a packet of money. He starts to hand it over but then draws back. "I don't know," he says, voice hesitant. "I've put a lot of faith into this arrangement with Anex and to just accept this... well that means I'm accepting bad practices."

"It shouldn't happen again." It *shouldn't*, but I'm not convinced. Anex is expanding too fast. Moving to territories where we don't understand the culture or know the people. He's brought in more of young men in the community—giving them access and jobs they aren't prepared for. That's how this mistake happened. One of our men, Malen, fucked up.

I glance into the shop front and see Imogene holding a piece of melon in her fingertips and quietly speaking to the woman. "I'll personally make sure of that."

The man chuckles. "That's not as comforting as you think it is son."

My jaw tightens. "Then what would smooth this over? This

partnership is important to Anex and to the community of Serendee. Tell me, what's it going to take to make this right."

He reaches up and rubs the tip of his chin with two fingers. His beard is thick, long. His nails dirty. "Rumor has it there's other merchandise for sale in your community."

I blink trying to follow. There's the herbal trade, the salves Silas makes and uses. A group of women harvest honey and wax, along with other products from the hives. There's dairy and of course, the produce, which he already seems to have in supply. I frown. "What merchandise are you speaking of."

He pulls back the burlap curtain and nods inside. "Property like that little thing in there."

"Women?" I blurt.

"Girls. Females." He says it with zero emotion, completely business-like. "The community I belong to… we've recently changed our decrees to include polygamy and we have too many men. We need more females."

"You want to buy her." It's a statement. One I manage to keep controlled despite the rage building inside. "From me."

"From Serendee. Anex has made it known this is a service he plans on providing soon." He tilts his head toward Imogene. "If you want to make things right between us, you'll give me that one as a peace offering."

I'm not sure how to describe the sensation that runs through me. It's white hot, searing straight from my soul. I only know one thing and it's that I will slaughter anyone that dares touch—to possess—Imogene other than me and my brothers.

My gun is out of the waistband of my pants before Jeb even blinks. The barrel two inches from his forehead.

"Woah," he says, holding up his hands, one still holding the packet of money. "Settle down, big boy, if that one is your toy, let me know. I'll pick another one."

I take a step in the small doorway and say, "Little Lamb, get in the truck."

"What?" she says, but then I hear a small gasp. She must've seen the gun. "Elon what—"

"Get in the truck, *now*."

I hear more than see her leave the rickety building. Her feet shuffle across the hay floor and the heavy truck door opens and shuts with a slam. Once she's safe, I cock the trigger. "I don't know what you heard or have been told about the women in Serendee but you've been given the wrong impression." Jeb swallows, his scraggly beard dipping to touch his chest. "Our women are sacred, prized possessions to be honored and worshipped." The words are what I've been told a thousand times sitting at Anex's feet, listening to hours of his lectures. But they taste bitter on my tongue. It's what we preach, but not what we practice. "Take your product," I say, shoving the basket at him and then snatching the money out of his hand. I'd leave it, but then I'd have to tell Anex why I came home empty handed. "And be thankful I'm not blowing your brains out." Jeb's eyes close when I unlatch the trigger, the click loud in both of our ears. "If I find out you're buying women from anyone else, I'll be back. Understand?"

He nods slowly, and I step away, keeping my gun trained on him and then the woman at the counter. She's hunched down, tears running down her face. I wonder if she knows how disgusting this man is.

Quickly, I get to the car, slamming the door and cranking up the engine with a deafening roar. I'm backed out and a mile away before I start breathing again.

"What happened?" Imogene asks.

"It was just a reminder that people aren't always what they seem." I grab her hand, threading my fingers with hers, and lift it, kissing the back.

She stares at me with a million questions in her eyes. I have no idea how to answer them because I have too many of my own.

18

____

I mogene

I CAN'T GET anything out of Elon as he speeds away from the farm stand and drives to a nearby town. He hasn't let go of my hand, steering the car one handed, the muscle at the back of his jaw ticking. All I know is whatever happened back there shook him up. As the miles pass, I can't help but look at the packet he left on the seat between us. It's thick with money—money that goes back to Anex.

He'd looked so different back there. Sure, he was strong and powerful. Commanding. Seeing him with the gun in his hand sent a thrill down my spine. Fear. Awe.

But it was the way he told me to run—the plea for my safety— that felt different. The look in his eye wasn't hard and angry. It was soft and kind. Elon cares about me. And not just because I belong to his best friend. A strange feeling swirls in my belly as we drive over a bridge marked with a sign announcing that we're entering Thistle Cove, home of the Vikings, the state football champions.

"Have you been here before?" I ask, desperate to break the silence.

"A couple times. There are just a few small dealers in the area. We keep them supplied."

My whole life has been nothing but inside the walls of Serendee and the short trip to the Center once I got a job. Seeing all of these other places, it's like visiting another world.

The town is small but cute and Elon quickly finds the public library. He parks the truck and says, "Just stick close to me, okay?"

I nod and wait as he exits the driver's side and walks around to open my door, helping me down from the oversized truck. Our skin sparks when it touches, and his fingers linger, tangled with mine.

He looks down at our hands and pulls away, allowing mine to fall. Clearing his throat, he asks, "You said you needed to check social media sites?"

"Yes." I follow him up the sidewalk to the library door. "Well, that's what Rex called it. I kind of know what it is from my training sessions with Silas—the entertainment he showed me, but I don't know how to navigate it at all."

Social media, or how I understand it, is places on the computer where people can talk and meet each other.

"Who is he looking for that he couldn't do it himself?" he asks as we walk into the cool, quiet building. A librarian observes us walk in, probably aware that we're not from around here. A row of computer sits along one wall. Elon presses a hand into my lower back and directs me toward them and pulls out a chair for me. I sit and he grabs another chair, setting it close to mine.

My palms sweat at his question. What I'm asking him to participate in... well, it's going to make whatever happened back at the farm stand seem minor.

"He wants me to find my mother."

Just saying those words are enough to have me labeled as Regressive and sent down with the Fallen—after intense Corrections and public reprimand. It's a testimony of how much I trust Elon that I would ask him to help me with something like this.

"I assume this is really about *his* mother?" He asks. I nod and he just sighs, running his hand through his thick, dark hair. "And this is the rabbit hole he's going down. Fucking great."

He pulls the keyboard toward him and starts typing. A screen pops up that says, 'Facebook' and I watch as he types in a familiar, forbidden name, Camille Sanders.

Before I can breathe, a photo pops up. It's both familiar and not. The eyes are the same, and the mouth, but the hair is short and graying. There are wrinkles and a lift to her chin—a confidence.

I grab the machine and twist it in my direction, touching the screen with my fingers.

"That's—"

"Her. Yes. I remember what she looked like."

I squint trying to absorb everything. I push his hand off the mouse and frantically try to make it comply. It spins out of control. "I just want to make it bigger!"

"Shhhh!" the librarian shushes from across the room. Elon's hand closes over mine, warm and heavy. He helps orient the mouse and clicks on her picture. It takes us to a page with limited information.

"Is that it?" I ask, speaking over the lump in my throat. "Is there nothing else?"

"It's a private account, which, frankly, is smart." He clicks around a little more but doesn't make much progress. "If you want to speak to her directly, you'll have to make an account and engage her."

The suggestion hits my chest like a battering ram. "Everything you just said is a violation."

He nods. "It is."

My hands shake and I put them in my lap. Again, he clamps his over mine and a feeling of calm follows. "If you do this, Imogene, you can't Correct this out of your system. You'll be crossing a line that comes from being part of Anex's inner circle. One you can't come back from, and one," he lowers his voice, "you can't have Levi take out of your hide with a strap."

"What do you mean?"

"I mean, you make a decision. You're either a sweet little lamb that follows The Way, or you're one of us."

I look up at his handsome, intimidating face. "Who are you?"

"The Chosen. We're not exactly *above* the rules and Corrections, but there's a gray area. That's where the four of us exist."

"I don't know if I can do that." Give up everything I know—the rules and belief system—The Way.

He squeezes my hand. "It's okay if you can't, but I need you to understand your limits. Because you can't keep punishing yourself for our Lapses."

"I don't know if I can separate the two."

He watches me closely, his dark eyes drinking me in, like he's trying to see inside my mind, how it works. "How about this," he says. "I'll do the research. Take down the information. If you want it, I can tell you, but it's my burden. My Lapse. Not yours." His eyes flick down to my mouth and back up. "And if you need me to, I'll go to Corrections to make it right."

It's a generous offer, and one that, like he said, wades into the gray water of our world. But at this point I don't any other option. It's a lifeline.

I take it.

"Okay, let's try that."

He takes the keyboard back and types quickly, faster than I would've thought possible. He enters in my mother's name. "Grab that flyer," he says, nodding to a stack on a nearby table. He pulls a pen out of his pocket. I watch as he jots down addresses and strings of phone numbers. He's quiet, but thorough, sliding the paper over to me when he's finished.

"I think she lives or works at one of these addresses. It's hard to tell—she's good at covering her tracks."

I stare at the information, trying to reconcile it with the years of her absence.

"You okay?" he asks, knee nudging mine.

"My mom, Camille, has been gone so long. I guess I didn't think it would exist." I lift up the paper. "But here it is and I guess I just don't know what to do with this?"

"Give it to Rex?"

"Do you think I should?"

"Wasn't that the plan?" he asks.

"Yes, but... I guess I didn't think it would be this easy or maybe even possible. Or..."

"Or what?"

"Or maybe I hoped she was dead and that's why she never came back for me."

"Anex wouldn't have let her come back, you know that."

I do know that, right?

"He would've put her in with the Fallen," he continues. "She would have been punished severely for her betrayal. Banishment was a mercy."

I take a deep breath, trying to steady myself. "Is there anything else we can find out first? Like does she have a job. Or," I swallow, "a family or something."

He looks at me for a long moment. My cheeks burn. "Sure, let me see what I can find."

His fingers move fast, entering in different variations of my mother's name and certain words. 'Keywords.' He pauses over something, and I sense his shoulders tense. "What?" I ask leaning over.

"There's a link to a group." He clears his throat. "It's for survivors of cults."

Cult.

Serendee is not a cult.

The people who say that do not understand who and what we are. They can't comprehend the community we've created. They view us as a threat. The self-sustainability, the progress and Enlightenment. Anex has always said that people who think we are a cult are missing out on the truth of The Way.

Yet...

I stare at my mother's face in a photo on the website. It's a picture of her smiling, her hair short, and wearing secular clothing.

Under her photo is a caption. I close my eyes and say, "Read it. What does it say?"

Again, he clears his throat, his foot bouncing on the floor. *"Camille Sanders spent decades in a cult that she not only willingly joined but helped create. She brings that unique perspective to others when they are seeking freedom from a controlling group..."*

"Stop."

Elon pauses. "Imogene."

"I can't do this." I stand, leaving the paper on the table and walk toward the door. "Rex will be upset." Furious. "But I can't do this. If he wants to dig around in this blasphemy, he has to do it on his own."

I step outside, letting the warm afternoon sun hit my face. I stand there until Elon is behind me, leading me back to the car. My chest is tight all the way back to Serendee, where I expect to finally breathe easy until we're back home, safe behind the walls.

For the first time in my life, there is no comfort.

I TRY my best to pretend like everything is normal.

Normal.

As residents of Serendee we've spent our lives pushing back on that word. Rebelling against the status quo. We're Better. More Enlightened. But the more I learn about the outside world, the less 'normal' make sense.

Is it normal to live in a community that sells illegal drugs?

Is it normal to have young girls kept in seclusion for re-education?

Is it normal to maintain your diet, clothing, hygiene all by the order of one man?

Everything I'm taught says yes.

Which is why the slip of paper Elon wrote my mother's information on burns where I've hidden it under my clothing, against my chest.

I haven't given it to Rex yet. He wasn't home last night when we returned. He'd left a note about working late down at the farm. It was dawn when he came in, undressed and crawled into the bed next to me, asleep in seconds.

I've been at work for three hours—greeting new recruits. Handing out paperwork and scheduling appointments. Normal stuff. A normal day.

I pretend the paper isn't there.

"How much did you say the next level costs?"

I smile at the girl across from my desk. She's a thin brunette that Rex recruited from the Wittmore campus. Over the last three months she's depledged from her sorority, come to three different workshops and is ready to commit to more. One of my jobs is to help the recruits level-up, paying for the courses that help them transition to Enlightenment. Once they pass through all the levels, they are slowly transitioned into potential community members. That's where Silas' skills come in—then Anex.

This girl, Brianna, is months away from that place—years even —but I can already see the gleam in her eye. She's hooked—high on the coursework and potential. She wants to Be Better, so much she can taste it.

"Five thousand," I tell her. The fee is part of other commitment. Anex only wants the most devoted to get to the higher levels. It's an important phase of the system. I look down at her paperwork. She's a college student with no income of her own but her mother is an architect. A quick skim of her financials, which we run after the second session, and it's obvious that her family has the type of resources Anex prefers.

"That's a lot," she says, twisting her fingers. There's a tan line on her ring finger. She'd been engaged when she first started coming. Is that over now? "I can probably swing some of it. Do you have a payment plan?"

"There are some options," I say, knowing this woman ticks all the boxes of the potential recruit Anex is interested in. "You know, I think you have the kind of energy Anex is looking for. Let me show him your file and see what he says about finding you a way into the next levels."

Her eyes brighten. "That would be amazing. I'm getting so much out of the courses, I'd hate to stop now."

"I understand," I say, giving her an assuring smile. I can't help but wonder what Rex did to get her in the door. Did he flirt with her? More?

I shake that off and tell her to come back the following day—that I'd let her know about funding. Gathering the file, including a recent photo of Brianna, I take it to the back. There's a small area outside of Anex's office, prepared to leave it in the mail slot for important papers. I've just slid the papers inside when the office door opens.

"I thought I heard someone out here." His eyes rake down my body, eliciting a chill that runs down my spine. "I didn't expect it to be my son's beautiful future mate."

"Anex," I say, bowing and touching my forehead. "I didn't know you were in the office."

"I snuck in the back," he says holding his finger up to his lips. "Shhh, don't tell anyone."

It's that kind of informality that makes Anex such a compelling leader. He's easy—approachable. It's also why I'm conflicted by imaginary weight on my chest. That note could destroy me and the guys. I laugh, hoping it doesn't sound nervous. "I was just leaving a file for you. A potential recruit, level three, that doesn't have the funds to proceed. She fit the criteria you requested for review."

"Thank you, Imogene. You're so thorough." His smile wavers. "I wish some of your diligence and dedication would rub off on Rex."

I still, not sure how to respond to the statement. Do I agree and criticize both my mate and his son? Or do I laugh it off, pretending it's a joke. The glint in his eye, the same blue eyes that Rex has tells me it wasn't in humor.

Before I dwell too much on it, I say, "I wanted to thank you for

Ordering us together. Although it's been a challenge working through our differences, lately things have been good."

His eyebrow raises. "Really?"

"Yes. He seems more focused and efficient. He comes home at night instead of spending time outside of Serendee." In clubs and parties. All of that is true. "I feel good about the match."

"I like hearing that."

"You chose wisely," I tell him, hoping the flattery works.

"I've been wanting to speak to you," he says, "Do you have time now?"

It's a question but there's no possible way to say no. Not to Anex.

"Of course. Melody is up front. She can handle anyone that comes in."

He gestures for me to enter his office. I've been here before—but just for a few moments. Before I was Ordered to Rex my interaction with Anex was rare—I probably saw him a little more since I work at the Center but even then, it's not as if he mingles with us. He's busy. I didn't understand the enormity of the businesses being run out of Serendee until Elon showed me. What we really sell and trade to keep the community running.

I enter the room and although I expect him to sit behind his desk he doesn't, leaning against the edge and crossing his legs in front of him. I watch as he reaches for a box on the table and pulls out a small hand wrapped cigarette. He doesn't speak as he strikes a match, the smell of sulfur hitting my nostrils. He lights the end and takes a drag.

"Have you ever?" he asks.

"Um..." Me? I glance over my shoulder—waiting for something. But what? I'm with Anex. Nothing can happen to me here. "No. It wasn't allowed in the Domum."

"I'm shocked my son and his friends haven't introduced you."

They haven't. And for a moment it makes me wonder why? Do they not trust me?

He tilts his head. "Your mind is running wild, isn't it?" He laughs. "So like your mother. Always thinking. Scheming."

The sensation of something creeping up my spine keeps me rigid, that and the fact that I have the notes about my mother under two thin layers of cotton. Is this meeting more than it seems?

God.

Does he know?

It's insane to think, but Anex has his ways.

It's the paranoia of any kind of resistance that makes me admit, "It's hard for me to turn my brain off sometimes. I don't know why. I think it's all those years of worrying—of being considered different."

"Because of Camille." He nods. "I can imagine. She was a powerful person."

Was.

She no longer exists in this world. We may as well be speaking of the dead, but the paper against my chest, the evidence on the computer last night. My mother isn't dead. She's alive and actively working against Serendee.

"Don't worry, Imogene. Other than that, you're nothing like her." He reaches out, brushing his fingers down my cheek and tucking a strand of hair over my ear. "You don't think I'd let a female with a true Regressive streak mate with my son, would you?" His hand lingers for a moment, trailing down my neck, before he steps back and takes another hit, before offering it to me. "You should try it. Take the edge off."

The pressure is intense. I reach for the tiny twist of paper.

"Ah," he says, withdrawing it a little. "Let me."

He holds it to my mouth, leaving just an inch for me to press between my lips. Awkwardly, I bend forward, inhaling the sweet herbal grass. As the smoke drags into my lungs it burns, spreading across my chest. I try to hold it in, but I cough, my throat raw.

"I'm sorry," I say, sputtering.

"It happens," he says. "Just takes a little practice." He leans forward again, pressing the joint to my lips. I have no choice but to inhale. When I pull away, he looks at me, eyebrow lifted. "You've been practicing, right?"

"Practicing?"

"With Elon, Silas, and Levi. Practicing to be an appropriate mate for my complicated son."

Anex is fit—mostly from the hours of nightly basketball games and his healthy lifestyle. He's vegan, meditates, practices yoga. His personal healer is always on call. Like Rex, his frame is imposing, muscular, and no matter how friendly his tone, there's something intimidating about him—always.

"I, uh…" Be it the question or the cannabis running through my system, it's hard to formulate words.

"I know all of this is new for you, Imogene. Exposing yourself like this—after the years of modesty and decorum." He sits on the edge of the desk. "I know it doesn't seem fair, but the males…we allow them more freedom so that when it's time for you to enter your mating, someone understands how things work. My son is more aware than most. He's experienced the decay and desperation of the outside world. It has left him hollow. I should have protected him more—especially without a mother." He smiles gently. "That's one reason I thought maybe you two would connect—the lack of a mother."

"It has," I say, tongue feeling looser. "It's been an adjustment for both of us.

"What kind of things do they ask you to do… they do ask you? Or do they force you?"

My stomach twists. The look in his eye conveys something darker, deeper—hunger.

"Do they hurt you, Imogene? Or do you only like to be hurt during your Corrections?"

The question shocks me—I'm aware that Anex has access to our logs and journals. That Levi reports to him, but has he told him about that? About my desires? How the pain and pleasure turn into one?

"You're such a good girl," he says, words thick. Or are my ears thick? "You've always been a good girl, Imogene, even when you're feeling bad."

"I—"

He rests his hand on my shoulder, the weight heavy, pressing me down.

"Ask me."

"For what?" I whisper.

"For a blessing."

I've done this before. Everyone in Serendee has been blessed by Anex—it's an honor—one we usually receive at ceremonies. I bend my knees, resting them on the hard floor. He stands above me, my eyes level with the seam of his crotch. Never before has it been like this—with his erection bulging against the fabric. Or if it was, I didn't know what I was looking at.

God, I was so naïve.

No one touches you without my permission.

I hear Rex's voice as his father's hand comes down on my head. He murmurs, words I can't fully make out: *girl, Enlightenment, The Way, peace and succumb.* Rambling on as his hand moves, cupping my cheek and lifting my chin.

"Is there anything you need to confess to me?" he asks. "Anything weighing on you?"

He knows. He knows about Elon and the computer. The search for my mother. The information we have. He knows and he'll use it against me and I open my mouth to tell him everything. I close my eyes, listening to the thrum of my pulse in my ears, my chest, feeling his thumb graze over my bottom lip.

This is wrong—he is wrong. I do not belong to him. I belong to Rex. To Elon, Silas, and Levi.

I understand that more than ever.

But this man is my leader, he has been my entire life, and no matter how scared I am, or how wrong this feels, I'm frozen under his power. He tilts my face upward and I look into his eyes—wincing at the similarity with his son. Except there's something missing—the deep intensity that Rex and I share. The connection.

What I see in Anex's face is disturbing want—the same kind that sent the blood rushing to his erection. I know that look now. I understand it from my training. Anex doesn't view me as a member of the community—or his son's mate. He sees me as something he wants *physically*.

My breath catches and his other hand shifts, moving to the front of his pants. It's in those mere moments I see my future flash before me. Anex forcing himself on me. Rex discovering it. The fallout. Bloodshed. Loss. Destruction.

Footsteps echo in the hallway outside the door, breaking me from the spell. What I can only describe as The Way, surges through me and I jolt to my feet.

"Thank you," I mumble, cheeks hot. Anex doesn't move, doesn't react as I race from the room, ignoring Melody dropping paperwork into his mail slot.

I run, passing my desk, out into the streets. I don't stop until I'm at the path that leads back home and only then do I stop to retch, the contents of my stomach, of my *soul*, trying to flee my insides. Nothing about me is good, or better, and soon the whole of Serendee will find out, and what will I do then?

19

___

L^{evi}

The creak of the door wakes me, followed by the sliver of light that vanishes with the sound of the latch sliding in place. I sit up and blink, "Who's there?"

"It's me." Her voice is quiet. Small.

"Imogene." I rub my eyes, trying to rouse myself. "What are you doing? What time is it?"

"Late," she replies, her voice closer. "I couldn't sleep."

"How come?" I'm groggy. The day had been long—filled with courses and a game of basketball that lasted past 3 AM.

"I can't stop thinking about all of the Lapses I've accumulated over the last few days. All of the Indulgences. The Regress—" The violations rush from her, like a dam breaking under pressure.

"Stop." I sit all the way up, the mattress squeaking under my weight. In the dark I feel for her, fumble for her hand, and pull her to the bed. "Sit."

The bed sinks, warmth brushes against my leg. I pull back, cock already hardening. What man hasn't had fantasies of a beautiful woman coming to him at night. My blood pumps through my extremities, but there's a hard truth mixed with it. She doesn't want me—she wants what I dole out—punishments.

"Talk to me," I say, my eyes finally acclimating to the moonlight coming through my window. "Tell me what's going on."

She shifts, hands clasped in her lap. She's not wearing a cotton, Serendee approved nightgown, but a Rex approved nightie, lace and satin. The soft brush of light highlights the swell of her breast and holy—my balls clench.

"It started when Rex asked me to do some research for him." She tells me about what Rex wants. Information on her mother, Camille, so that he can search for the truth about Beatrice. Like a breeched dam, the information pours out of her, the revelations spoken in whispers, only revealed in the dark.

I understand why. If anyone is going to report her back to Anex, it will be me. And admittedly, the impulse is strong. The urge to run to the Main House and tell our leader all of the darkness, all of the deceit screams in my veins. I was raised to be an informant.

But the woman sitting on the bed, hands fisted in her flimsy skirt, tugs at something deep in my chest. "I haven't told Rex yet. I've barely seen him, but today I had the information on me at the Center and Anex called me in." Her voice wobbles. "He could have caught me, Levi. Then what?"

"He didn't," I say, terrified for her. If he'd found that information on her. Christ. She'd be with the Fallen right now. Or worse. Banished. "He didn't, that's all that matters."

"There's more," she adds. "He offered me cannabis. I took it. I had no choice."

"It's not against the rules of Serendee to smoke—especially with the leader."

Her eyes drop. "He was familiar with me. He touched me—"

"Where?" My tone is sharp. Harsh.

"Nothing inappropriate." She glances up, eyes wary. "Not really. It felt inappropriate. I *know* Rex would be angry."

I take a deep breath. She's right. Anex's interest in Imogene has surpassed appropriateness. But what is considered appropriate where he's concerned. He establishes the rules—the boundaries. I reach out and touch her cheek and hear myself say, "It's okay, Imogene. It's going to be okay."

"It's not," she says, through a quiet, shuddering sob. "Asking Elon to take me there, looking it up on the computer, reading all the blasphemous, Regressive thoughts my mother is spewing. Maybe I do need to be Re-Educated." She looks up at me, eyes shining. "Maybe I should be with the Fallen."

Maybe she should.

No. *No.* That's years of conditioning saying that. Not The Way.

"She called Serendee a cult," she continues, the words are barely a whisper. More breath than voice. "Please, Levi. I'm trying to be a good mate to Rex and give him what he needs, but it's tearing me apart." She presses against me, her the fullness of her breast against my arm. "Please help me become whole again. Show me The Way. Help me seek Enlightenment."

If I give her what she wants, then we can both be saved. Her from her Lapses and me from having the knowledge. But every time Imogene comes to me like this, my motives become convoluted. Slippery like sand. My brain doesn't rule my decisions, but the hard, throbbing want in between my legs. Imogene isn't the only one drowning, being pulled between what's Right and what Feels Good.

But that's not all. Anger courses through me. Hot and dangerous. How could Rex put her in this position. Put Elon and then me? What the hell is he thinking?

And Anex... would he dare covet his son's mate? Would he cross that line by getting her high and loose? The answer rises faster than I want to admit. *Yes.* Yes, he would.

Rage born of confusion and conflict flickers and my fists tighten. It would be so easy to take this out on another—on

Imogene. I could tear her skin apart, use her to quell the storm building in my soul.

So easy to hurt her.

So easy to ruin her.

Her fingers touch my chin and force my eyes to hers. "Levi?"

"I won't."

"Won't what?"

"Can't." My limbs tremble. "This is how he destroys us. It's how he pits us against one another and allows evil to worm further under our skin."

"Who are you talking about."

I stare at her, unable to say his name, fearful of being struck down by some greater force, but I see the understanding flicker in her eyes. She knows. Anex.

"He's the one that wants me to... Correct you like this. The escalation. The strap. He wants you fearful and weak." I swallow. "It's why he invited you into his office today. He doesn't know about the information. If he did, the recourse would be swift and public. He wouldn't play games." I shift on the mattress, getting closer to her. "He may suspect something, but he was fishing."

"Are you sure?"

No. "Yes."

"That doesn't take away everything else," she says, although she looks relieved. "The need for Correction. It's The Way and despite everything, I still believe."

I shake my head. There's a part of me that wonders if this isn't part of Anex's plan. To make her uncomfortable. To have her Lapse, and then come to me to start this cycle over again. It sucks us both in, keeps us both complicit, hungry. Horny.

"I'm worried we're going too far—that Anex wants us to go too far. Everyone logs in their journals. Confesses and shows some penance, but where this has gone..." I swallow. "It's eating away at me. Inside and out."

"You don't like it? You don't want to do it?"

I brush her hair off her cheek. "No, Imogene, I want it too much.

So much it scares me. The things I want to do to you. How I fantasize about treating you. It can't be right."

My brain hurts. My arms and legs ache. My stomach churns.

'She called Serendee a cult.'

Camille Sanders Montgomery is notorious for being a lot of things, but I've seen the records, the history and foundation of her work building Serendee. At one point she was a believer and hearing that she has used that term to describe us rocks my foundation. If someone like that can change her mind, what does that mean for the rest of us?

Imogene shifts next to me, lifting up the covers and sliding her legs in next to mine. It's an act of softness, tenderness and it's in direct opposition of how we treat one another. She must know it, because her limbs remain tense as our bodies draw together, like two magnets. She tucks against my side, pulling my arm around her shoulders. Unsure of what else to do, I rest my other hand on her belly.

"What if she's right?" I ask. "What if we're just being manipulated and controlled?"

It's the thing Rex has fought with his father about for years, but even he's too under his thumb to really leave.

"Then our whole lives are a lie," Imogene says, pressing her lips against my collarbone. "But what's worse? Living the lie or breaking free?" She sits up. "What would you rather do? Pretend nothing is wrong and keep living this life or go out there? Live in the secular world with their noise and dirty streets and crime? Maybe it's just the price we have to pay?"

She leans toward me, her tits round and full. I cup one with my hand, running my thumb over the nipple. I've only touched her like this once without inflicting Correction—pain. And there's a disconnect between my mind and body. She grabs my hand and places it over her breast, applying pressure.

"Make me pay, Levi," she says, grinding against my thigh. My cock swells. "Help me reconcile my actions."

She wants it hard. She wants pain with her pleasure. It's mixed up and confusing, but in the darkness of this room, it doesn't have to belong to anyone but us. Anex may have made this monster, but I'm the one releasing it from its cage.

"Are you sure?" I ask, because I feel the same pull.

"Yes." She nods, taking my hand and pushing it between her legs. It's hot. Wet. Ready. "I've been a very bad girl."

I rise up, shifting from the unsure, insecure man who doesn't know what to do with a woman in a bed, to the one that understand this specific language. This desire.

I already know what I want to do to her. I've been waiting for her to return. I knew she would. It was a matter of *when*, not *if*.

"Lay back," I tell her, and she arranges herself on the bed, head on the pillow. Opening the drawer on the bedside table, I pull out the hard, heavy object. The handle nestles in my palm. Imogene watches me with wide, worried eyes, a line creasing her forehead. I lick my bottom lip.

"What's that for?" she asks, a tremble in her voice when she sees the knife.

"Are you sure you want to know?"

She nods. "Yes."

In all the times we've been together I've never fully exposed myself to Imogene. I've kept on my clothes unless I've caved, spilling my cum on her back. She's been so honest with me, that I feel compelled. I hook my thumbs in my shorts and lower them, revealing myself.

I show her what I've been hiding all this time.

Her eyes dart my erection first, taking in my manhood, but then they slide to the side, to the flesh next to my hip. I don't look, ashamed of the wrath I've taken out on myself. She sits up, her fingers darting out. They touch the scarred skin, gentle and cool.

"You did this?" she asks, eyes darting to the blade in my hand. "With that?"

"Yes." Something feral unwinds in my chest, years of secret punishments. The only person that knows is Anex. "I'm allowed to do my own Corrections, as long as I log them in my journal."

She runs her thumb over the puckered skin, some scars run over time and time again. There are dozens, one for every Lapse, for every Regressive thought, for each Indulgence and every time I could Be Better and wasn't.

For every urge of pleasure, every ejaculation, every lingering desire I have after giving Imogene Corrections.

She's speechless, but I see the worry in her eyes. The pity. I swallow back my emotions and ask, "Do you trust me?"

Her nod is hesitant, but she doesn't run. Too bad, that's a game for another day.

"The normal way we'd do this is for me to give you a Correction for every Lapse." I unsheathe the blade, the silver glinting in the moonlight. "But this is about us. About release. I want you to tell me when you've had enough. When you're close... okay?"

"Okay."

Roughly, I spread her thighs, running my fingers over the creamy smooth skin. I know Imogene has a history of self-Correcting by cutting her flesh. This is another level of that. Pushing her panties aside, I rub my fingers around the wet heat, watching her tremble, then I take the tip of the blade and press it into her inner thigh. I make the cut quick, guiding the blade down her inner thigh. Her legs quiver and I duck, lapping up the trail of blood with my tongue.

Her body is still, tense, frozen, and I wonder if I've gone too far, revealed too much of my darkness, but she drops her fingers to my head, curling them into my hair. "More."

I'm happy to oblige.

Again, I cut her, the thinnest of marks, the most delicious taste, coppery blood with the scent of her dripping pussy. When I lick her, her hips rise—seeking. I glance up her body, at her tits, and I see her nipples are hard, her free hand moves to it, tugging at the sharp peaks.

"How does that feel?" I ask her, the words a low grunt. My cock is blindingly hard, my mind delirious with lust. "Close?"

"Not yet," she says, spreading her legs wider. This time I don't cut her thigh but run the blade through the crotch of her panties. She gasps, eyes wide. I climb over her and flip the blade, nudging her pussy with the handle.

"You need more, don't you?"

"Yes." She nods, biting down on her bottom lip. I bend and capture her mouth, her tongue and press the handle of the knife into her. Her jaw drops and a small breath catches in her throat. Her hand lands on my forearm, the one holding the blade, and she squeezes the muscle as her hips rock forward. I plunge the handle in, knowing she wants it rough—raw—and give her what she needs.

"Oh!" I kiss her to swallow the cry. I thrust the handle in, fist dragging against her clit with every motion. "Harder," she begs against my mouth. "Fuck me harder, Levi."

I only wish I could do it with my cock, bury myself into her, pounding out every ounce of grief and rage and regret, but I don't deserve a woman like Imogene. She isn't *mine*. But I can give her what she needs, something Rex doesn't understand.

"Come for me, Imogene," I tell her, feeling her rising to the edge. "Let it go. Let go of the shame built up inside of you. Release all the pain." I keep away from the language of The Way, not wanting that to be what this is about. It's not about Lapses or Regression.

"I'm close," she says, and I slow my motion, dragging the handle in and out slowly, brushing my thumb over her clit. I bend, licking the trails of sticky blood off her inner thigh. It's that way, with my face between her legs and the knife pushed to the hilt that she finally comes, a deep guttural groan releasing all of the pent-up emotions she's been carrying.

I fist my cock, rock hard and a few strokes away from exploding and get to my knees. Imogene looks up at me, eyes glazed, fingers grazing my hipbone. "Let me—"

"No," I grunt. It's too late. I'm too far gone. I seize, back arching, jaw clenching, and come, thick ropey spurts of semen spilling on her thighs.

Our breathing slows and I look at us, truly look at the mess on the bed, the broken-down girl, the ripped panties and the blood and the semen. I don't know if I helped her or harmed her. Or what is up or down, if Anex is right or if we're all wrong.

One thing I'm pretty certain of, is that the two of us are fucking ruined, raw like a scabbed over wound I can't stop picking at.

Neither of us know how to stop making it worse.

"HE'S GOING to be mad when he sees these," she says, looking down at the wounds. "I don't know who he'll be angrier with, you or me?"

I grunt, fishing through the bedside table for a pot of Silas' salve. I find it, spinning open the top. She stopped bleeding a while ago, the cuts aren't that deep. I've learned the balance, how to manage the weight of the tip.

"I'll deal with Rex," I say, dipping my finger in the pot and scooping out a thick glob.

"It's okay. I can please him other ways."

I glance up at her mouth, imagining Rex's cock buried inside. Imagining *my* cock buried inside. I coat the cut with the salve and cover it with a bandage. "Keep it clean," I tell her. "But the knife is disinfected. It should heal okay."

Her hand rests on my hip, thumb rubbing the scars underneath my shorts. Regret washes over me. I shouldn't have shown her. It's my burden to carry, not hers.

"You know you can come to me, too," she says softly. "When you feel the urge to Correct."

I snort. "That's not how it's done."

Females do not Correct men. They don't have the disposition for it. They're too fair. It's the male's job to inflict, which is why Anex trusts us to do it to ourselves.

"I know it's not how it's done, Levi," she says, "but nothing we do here is by the book. We're all wandering through this together." Her voice lowers. "I'm worried about you. Those scars…"

"I shouldn't have shown you."

I move to stand, but her hand grabs my forearm. "Thank you for trusting me."

Trust.

I'd asked her to trust me, and I made her bleed and fucked her with a knife, yet here she is, pleading with me to let her in. Let her close.

I nod, but it's without conviction. There's no room for Imogene in my life. There is me, my faith and Anex.

Nothing else.

20

———

R^{ex}

It's been a week since I've seen my father, and it's not a surprise when I'm called to his rooms. I'd like to say there was some consistency, planned little meetings where my father checks in on the progress I'm making with the business or you know, just to check in on his son.

But no. Consistency isn't what makes Serendee tick. Not really. It looks like a well-oiled machine on the outside but under the surface, like the drugs and money, and sex and gluttony, is well-designed chaos.

It's how I've managed to keep Imogene so spun-out, so conflicted and confused. So willing to wear lace panties and go on birth control, to beg me to be in her bed at night. I've got her right where I want her and have no intention of stopping any time soon.

I step into the cool entryway of the Main House and start for the stairs.

"Rex."

Elon is standing right off the front hall.

"Hey," I say. "Going up to see, Anex."

He jerks his chin, indicating I should follow him. Huh. Curiously gets the best of me and when I get to the hallway he's nowhere around, but I stop, counting the wooden panels that make up the wall. I glance around, making sure no one is watching and tap on the top corner of one. It pushes back, revealing a small room.

"Wow," I say, looking around the cramped space. "It's been a while since we've been in here."

When my father built this house, he added in several secret rooms and passages, 'just in case.' No one in Serendee knows about them other than the closest of the inner circle. The guys and I used to use them for elaborate games of hide and seek or a spot to duck into when Anex was looking for us. Now, I look at my best friend and ask, "What's going on?"

"I don't even know where to start," he says, annoyance flickering across his face. "I got caught up in some bad shit yesterday making a delivery. Anex has us dealing with some shady people involved in even shadier shit."

I look at Elon closer. He's rattled. "What kind of shady shit?"

His lips purse together. "Imogene was with me, and the dirty old bastard tried to buy her from me."

Heat licks up my spine. "Jesus, Elon! Why the hell was she even with you?"

"Because I was taking her to run an errand for you." His finger jabs in my chest. He's a second from snapping but I don't give a shit. I am, too. "I thought it was a basic drop with some hippies or something. They were pissed Anex screwed him on the last drop off and wanted payment—in flesh."

"Son of a bitch." I rub my forehead, trying to wrap my head around everything he's saying. The fucked-up drug deal, I can get. Some of Anex's new recruits are sloppy and the business is growing too fast. But offering to buy my woman? Fuck no. "How did you leave it?"

"Without anyone getting killed, that's how. But it was fucking close."

"Why the hell would he presume Imogene was for sale?" I ask, trying to keep my anger in check. I know Elon would never knowingly put Imogene in harm's way, but every day living and working for my father is a dangerous pursuit.

"Yeah, that was my question, too. It was heavily implied that Serendee had expanded its services beyond selling weed. Apparently, he was under the impression we're trafficking women now."

Sex trafficking. I've spent enough time in the secular world to know we bend a lot of conventions in Serendee, but even that one doesn't sit well with me. Elon and I share a look, one that doesn't need to be spoken. There's no doubt who my father is using to build this trade, the ones he's already broken: The Fallen.

My chest is tight, caught up in the sheer insanity of what Elon is describing. I force myself to exhale, an attempt to control my rage. "She's okay?"

"Yes. I didn't tell her about the old guy trying to buy her, and she didn't see much of the altercation." His eyebrow rises. "She didn't tell you any of this?"

I shake my head. "No."

I'd come to bed last night as promised and passed out—hard. She was already out of the bed when I got up this morning.

"Then I guess she also hasn't told you about the dirt we dug up on her mother?" he asks.

I blink, again, trying to catch up. "That was the errand? You took her to find information about her mother?"

"Yes, asshole." His grim expression is back. "What the fuck are *you* thinking?"

"I'm thinking that woman may be the key to everything." I lean against the wall. "What did you find out?"

"She's hard to find, unless you dig deep enough, but the main takeaway is that Camille Sanders is very involved in an anti-cult group. One specifically focused on Serendee and your father."

Anti-cult.

The word rings in my ears. Cult. My father is many things, but a cult leader? Bullshit. That's just a word to discredit him and everyone in the community.

"There's more," he says. "And she doesn't know about it. I read all of the websites. Her mother has spent the last few years trying to get Imogene out of Serendee but has been unsuccessful."

"Trying how?"

Elon just shakes his head. "I don't know."

Possessiveness grips me. Get her out? As in remove her? Away from me? Fuck no. But I realize something else. I'm not the only one that won't let this girl get away from me. Neither would my father and the lengths he would go to in order to keep her here would far exceed my own.

"Thank you for coming to me, brother," I say, pressing my fingers into the wooden panel and open the door.

"What are you going to do?" Elon asks. He came to me for a reason, so that I could take care of this.

"I'm going to find out exactly what my father is up to."

I WALK past the guard and open the door leading to my father's rooms. My rank keeps anyone from stopping me or questioning my movements. There are no rooms, no sections of this community that are off limits to me.

I step inside the outer room of my father's luxurious suite and find the room empty. I make my way across the room, stopping at the bar to pour myself a drink. I need one after everything Elon told me. A loud bang from an adjacent room draws my attention, or rather a series of them, the thudding falling into a distinct rhythm, the unmistakable sound of fucking on the other side.

Guess I'll wait then.

I swallow the drink whole and am halfway through another when my father emerges from the bedroom, casually tying his linen robe. "Ah, son," he says, leaving the door ajar. I see three women in the bed, naked and looking well-fucked. Two I recognize from recruiting into Serendee myself. If my memory serves, she gives amazing head. "Sorry to keep you waiting, but my mates were in need of Enlightenment, and it's my duty to show them The Way."

I wonder if they truly are here on their own volition. The tactics I use during recruitment are heavy handed and determined. I don't take 'no' easily, and I'm as skilled at the art of persistence as Silas is with eating pussy. These thoughts piss me off, and I finish off my liquor.

"We're both here now," I say, lowering into one of the white chairs. "What did you call me up here for?"

He sits across from me and picks up a pipe on the coffee table. Carefully he packs the bowl, filling it with the strong-smelling herb piled in a ceramic pot. "Just catching up. We haven't spoken since the ceremony." He presses his thumb to the center of the bowl. "How is your mate?"

"She's fine," I say, leaning back, pretending I don't care that he's mentioning her. "Although a little rattled after the ambush she and Elon got into yesterday."

He hesitates, *slightly*, before resuming his task. "I don't know what you're referring to. Ambush?"

He probably doesn't, but I don't trust this man or his motives.

"One of our buyers was under the impression that we don't just deal weed, but that we also trade in flesh." I watch him closely. "And they tried to purchase Imogene."

Anex scratches a match across the side of a box and lights the pipe, taking a few short puffs before a long drag. He holds his breath, eyes watering, and then holds it out to me. I wave it off, controlling the urge of stabbing his eyes out with the mouthpiece.

"Did you hear me?" I ask.

"Yes, I heard you, and this sounds more like a matter of why Elon was parading your young, beautiful mate in front of noncommunity members. If you don't want people coveting your property, son, don't let it out of the gates."

"No," I say, shifting to lean closer, "that is not what happened. What happened is you're expanding our trade to people we don't know and cannot trust. *And* they are under the idea we sell women." Anex takes another long drag. "And I suspect there's truth to that, isn't there?"

He rests the pipe on the tray. "What are you implying?"

I glance toward the bedroom door where the women are still cuddled together on the bed. I don't hold back. "The women we bring in here. The ones you don't keep." I lift my chin. "The ones you lock up in the basement. The Fallen. You're selling them, aren't you?"

"Those women are in a re-education program that they've agreed to participate in. They're consumed by their Weakness, and I am simply trying to help them get back on the right path."

"To The Way," I state. I never noticed how my father spoke before he sent me out to recruit and deal to the frats in the University. How his words and terminology are specific to our community. I always felt like that elevated me, made me special. Better, but at some point, I realized it was just more mind games and manipulations.

I've heard this same tired rhetoric over and over again. My life has been filled with lectures and sermons and bullshit terminology, all of which leads back to him being in control, taking what he wants, *removing* the people that are a problem.

Like my mother. Like Imogene's.

The events of the last week come crashing down on me. The altercation with that prick, Miller, at the Zeta Sig house the other night—how he almost had his way with Imogene. And the situation with Elon, and later the details about her mother... how she's been trying to get her out. I'm bone tired and my patience has worn thin.

My father isn't a cult leader—he's a conman.

"If you're asking if I'm expanding our business opportunities, the answer is yes. Our crops are booming, our reputation and product is stellar, and it's time to venture outside of Wittmore frat boys for buyers."

"And the women?"

He lifts his pipe and takes another drag. "The women are willing to do what it takes to attain Enlightenment."

"By whoring themselves."

Anex shrugs. "It's their nature, Rex. If you took the time to attend the men's group lessons, you would understand that." He leans back and regards me. "But I don't think you need a class to teach you about women. You inherited that trait from me, and even if you didn't, I think the actions of your betrothed should be enough evidence of what a woman will do if allowed sexual freedom with more than one man."

"This isn't about Imogene."

His head tilts. "Isn't it? Your mate can't keep her legs shut, son, and her darkness, it runs deeper than I could have ever anticipated. I knew she was a risk; her mother caused enough chaos when she lived here, but Imogene struggles on a different level."

I think about the lashes and the Correction she craves so much —the way she goes to Levi to inflict it. She's devoted, but strong-willed. She's lost—but claimed. Years of living under my father's control has left her with a mind so fucked up that she's barely any different than the women downstairs, locked in those tiny cells.

"She is mine to deal with," I say, voice low and even. "And what happens in my house, with my woman, is not your business. You keep your mind and thoughts and manipulations away from her."

My father doesn't move, doesn't tense, or shift a muscle but I see the dark glint in his pupils, the flash of warning. "I'd watch your tone, son. Everything in Serendee is under my leadership. *Including* your mate. I gave her to you and just as quickly, I can take her away."

There's a menace under his words. An unspoken threat. *'Like your mother.'*

I stand, hands clenched tight at my sides. If they weren't, they'd be wrapped around his throat, choking the life out of him. The way he looks at me, with his chin lifted and his lips twisted smugly... it's almost a dare.

I walk away before I do something irreparable.

"Rex," he calls when I'm almost clear. I pause. "Tell your men the expansion is on. That'll mean longer hours and increased production, but that's a necessary sacrifice."

I turn slightly. "And the women?"

"That will be more discrete. I'll continue to prepare them for their next phase of Enlightenment and notify you and your friends when it's time."

"Fine," I say, swallowing back the thick bile rising in the back of my throat, but I don't let him see my disgust or horror. This is what my father does, who he is. He pushes us one step further, deeper, farther away from who we are as a community. As a people.

I'm afraid he'll push us so far one day we'll lose who we are entirely.

21

I mogene

I'M WALKING BACK from the Center when I see Elon go into the gym. I'm not sure why I follow him, but something urges me to follow.

The community gym is a hub in Serendee. Mostly for Anex's basketball games, but even when I lived in the Domum we would go for calisthenics and fitness class.

Today is the first time I've seen the soft flat mat in the middle. It's blue, with a red edging creating the impression of a box. I peer across the room at Elon as he drops his bag on a bench and pulls off his shirt, revealing his toned upper body. He reaches into his bag and pulls out a roll of something—tape, I realize as he wraps his knuckles.

Boxing. Or fighting. That's what this is.

There are other guys in the gym, but my focus is on Elon. His shoulders are wide, tapering down to his muscular chest and ripped abdomen that vanishes into a deep cut 'V' that travels under the waistband of his shorts. I didn't know men like this existed—or maybe I just never thought about it. We were kept so separate, so segregated.

My neck warms as I think about how this man has bent me over a table like a rag doll and pounded into me—releasing the buildup of pressure buried in my core. I wonder what it would be like to have him over me, all that muscle and deep-rooted anger.

I take a step back and let the fresh air just outside the gym, cool me off.

Elon doesn't want me like that. We've never had the intimacy that Rex and I have managed, or Silas with his sweet, caring nature. Even the connection I have with Levi is different... it's violent and all-consuming, but emotional.

At best I feel like Elon tolerates me. A means to an end. Another part of his job in Serendee. An obligation.

Thinking of it that way quells my urges. and I step back inside, curious about the fight.

Two men are on the mat now. Elon and one I recognize from around the community, Malen. He's leveled up lately, working closer to Anex. Wearing the all black clothing of members of his security.

He's also punching Elon in the face.

Shock ripples through me. Elon. Powerful, commanding and sure is getting his butt kicked by this other guy. He strikes him with his fist, his foot, his elbow and knee. Elon takes it, over and over, righting himself after each hit and gesturing for Malen to come at him again.

I step inside, closer, compelled to understand. There are others watching—all men—engrossed by the annihilation of one of Serendee's strongest.

Malen wipes the sweat from his forehead. "Had enough?"

"Nope," Elon says, spitting blood on the ground. "Another round." He looks at one of the guys waiting by the edge. "You, too."

Malen shrugs and bounces on his toes, waiting for the other man to walk into the ring. What I'm seeing feels unbelievable.

Watching Elon take on two men—while seemingly not fighting back.

Malen's elbow jerks back for another punch.

"What is happening?" I ask—out loud—although I mean to say it in my head. One of the other men looks back, eyebrows raised, surprised to see me.

"You're not supposed to be here," he says, but his tone isn't bossy. I see from his expression he recognizes me.

"What is this?" I ask, flinching when Elon takes another hit.

"None of your business, I imagine." The guy approaches me, putting his body between me and the ring.

I push him aside. "Stop!"

Elon's eyes jerk to the side at the sound of my voice. Just in time to snap away from Malen's fist slamming into his jaw.

"Stop!" I shout again. I rush past the guy blocking me and enter the ring. Malen's eyes widen when he sees me, his fists dropping.

"What is this?"

Elon's hands are on his knees, and blood drips to the mat. I can't tell if it's from his mouth or his eye. Maybe his nose.

"Stop," I breathe. "This has to stop."

"Go away, Little Lamb." Elon's voice is gruff, hard.

"No." I jerk my chin at Malen. "Go. Get out of here."

His lips curve. "Not sure it's your job to tell me what to do."

"You can do as I say, or I can go get my mate. Who would you rather deal with?" The way his spine straightens tells me he knows exactly who my mate is. "I thought so. Go." I look at the others. "You, too. Get out of here."

I drop down beside him and tentatively touch his shoulder. Once I hear the door slam, and I know we're alone, I ask, "Want to tell me what this is all about?"

"No." He rises up, shrugging me off. I don't back away though, worried about his face and head. His ribs. His mouth tugs down in a grimace and he limps off the mat.

"Elon! What is this? What are you doing?"

He turns. It's slow and looks painful. "I'm doing what I said I would." His eyes dart to the mat, now covered in blood. "Those were my Corrections."

I blink, remembering how he'd promised me he would take Corrections for finding the information on my mother. He was assuming my guilt—my Lapse.

I had no idea he'd do it this way.

"Are you crazy? You could get seriously hurt!"

"Me?" He's shoulders shift back and he strides toward me. "I'm trained. I spent years learning how to fight and defend myself. But what about you? About the beatings you take from Levi to assuage your guilt? The assault you call Enlightenment?"

"It's not the same. You weren't fighting back."

"Neither do you." His eyes narrow—or they try. The left one is swollen and puffy. He looks unsteady on his feet. I don't think, I just wrap my arm around his waist.

"I'm fine."

"Okay, sure." He doesn't resist when I help him over to the bench, although to be fair, he outweighs me by at least a hundred and twenty pounds. "Sit."

For once in his life, he follows directions, sighing heavily as he eases to the hard seat.

"Wait here."

I head to the back room—a small kitchen, I've been in while serving refreshments at the basketball games. There's an ice machine and a stack of clean towels. I fill the towel with ice and wet a few others in the sink. When I come back out, he's on his back, the hard bench aligned with his spine. I bend down to my knees, pressing the ice to his swollen eye. "Hold this."

"You're awfully bossy today," he says, keeping the ice in place.

"Well, I think Malen knocked your good sense out around the third punch."

He laughs, but it's lacking any real levity. He winces and groans.

"How often do you do this?" I ask, wiping the blood off his chin.

His eyes meet mine. "Not often. Corrections are something I gave up a long time ago."

"So, why now?"

"Because I promised." He looks away. "And because I put you in harm's way and that deserved some consequences." It may be the most honest thing he's ever said to me and my heart aches because I'm the one that drove him to this.

I stand, leaving the cloth on the bench. Bending, I grab the hem of my skirt and lift it. His eyes widen as I reveal myself. If he questions it, he never speaks. This isn't about sex or lust or anything else. It's about showing my scars, the way he just showed his. I know when he sees them. His eyes widen, lips turn down. His hand shoots out and he grabs me by the back of the thigh, pulling me close.

"Who did this?" His thumb grazes under the red, scabbing wound. It's ugly, like I feel inside.

I swallow, heat burning my cheeks. "Levi, but only because I asked him to."

Begged.

He rises up, spinning his legs until he's sitting up and facing me. His hand fists in my skirt, and he pulls me close.

"I don't like it," he grunts.

I touch the side of his face, grazing his puffy eye, the result of his own Correction. "Are you sure?"

"That's different. I don't like it when you hurt yourself." He kisses the healing cuts. Each one. Slow and gentle. "Your skin is perfect. Soft. You're perfect."

I thread my fingers in his hair, lifting his face to mine. "I'm anything but."

"I guess that's why we like you then, because neither are we."

His hands slide up my skirt, hiking my foot up on the bench. He kisses the scar again, but pushes his fingers underneath my panties. He rubs against my clit, sending shockwaves deep to my core. "You like it?" he asks.

"Mmhmm."

"You're getting wet for me, aren't you?"

I nod, biting down on my bottom lip. My pussy is inches from his face, my foot is planted on the bench. He rubs tiny circles against my nub, until my breath is labored and if he doesn't stop I'll come like this, right on his hand.

"Elon," I warn. "I'm going to—"

He drops his hand and drags me onto his lap. I feel him beneath me—hard and eager. He shudders, and I think it's from pain, but when his eyes meet mine, I sense it's something deeper.

Maybe Elon and I have a connection after all.

I kiss him gently, taking care not to bruise his already busted lip, he doesn't seem to care, coming at me hard, fingers digging into my skin like he's trying to claw his way inside. Between my legs, he yanks my panties to the side, brushing his fingers over the sensitive, pooling heat. I shiver and confess, "That feels so good."

"Everything about you feels good, Imogene." He kisses my throat. "*Everything.* Your skin. Your body. Your pussy." His finger sinks in when he says it, eliciting a cry. "So tight and wet. I just want to bury myself inside of you, fill you up until you can't take it anymore."

"Do it," I say, it's less of a challenge than a plea. "I want to feel you, too."

My heart hammers and my skin grows hot. Beneath the folds of my dress, he pulls out his erection. I can't see it, but I feel it, hot and steel-hard against my inner thigh, probing at my entrance. I wrap my hands around his neck and hold on as he impales me with his length, sinking down to take him as deep as I can.

He groans when our bodies connect, my forehead is dropped against my shoulder.

"You feel so good," he says, licking my collarbone. "So fucking good, Imogene."

I like the sound of my name on his tongue and lift his head so I can kiss him. Tongues tangled, his hips rock back and then forward, his hand sliding down my back to settle above my ass. He holds me there, thrusting into me. Channeling all that anger he had in the ring into me.

"I've told you before—stop hurting yourself. Come to me, I'll fuck that Lapse right out of your body." He jerks into me, pulling me with every thrust. I hold onto him, loving the feel of him inside —he's thick and stretches me with every invasion. I want him deeper, as deep as he can go and I raise my heels onto the bench next to him, "Oh," I say, as he grabs my ankles, pushing them behind his back. "Oh, that's it. *That's* it."

My clit rubs against him and what crests over me is unfamiliar —it's not laced with anger or regret. It's want and desire and true confession. It's something I've held inside of me for weeks, my real feelings for this real man, hard muscled and pounding into me. The orgasm comes at me like an impact, hard and dizzying, my breath caught in my throat and my nerves screaming from exposure.

"That's it, baby," he says, breath hot on my ear. "Come for me. Clench around me. Milk my cock. *Own* me."

He rises up with his final thrust, holding me against his body. His fingers dig into the flesh of my backside, his cock buried deep. Elon's orgasm comes with a roar, bouncing off the high ceilings, rattling deep in my chest. "Fuck, fuck, fuck, Imogene," he chants, each word accentuated with a punch, my pussy holding onto him like I never want to let go, because in this moment, it's us. There's no pain. Just feeling good. Feeling right.

Feeling a million miles away from this made-up world and the controls they have over us, I kiss him, wanting the feel of him linked to me last a little longer. The kisses are slower, longer, our chests rising and falling together as we come back to center.

"Promise me," he says, pulling back and cupping my cheek. He's still inside of me. I'm not ready to let go. "The next time you want to hurt yourself, let me try that first."

"Only if you do the same."

He nods, but there's something guarded in his eyes. A wariness, like he knows he can't keep his promise, even if he wants to. I don't push on because with the foundations of our upbringing and Anex's watchful eye, I can't either.

22

———————

I mogene

I'VE JUST COME in from work and am hanging my bag from the hook in the foyer when the door opens and Rex strides in. His shoulders are tight, his jaw set, and my stomach flip flops in worry about what he's upset about now. How much he'll make me pay for whatever has made him angry.

"We need to talk," he says, walking past me to the living room.

I follow him, nearly tripping over the hem of my skirt in the process. When I catch up I say, "You must be hungry—"going for the age-old lesson of feeding your man. They taught us this in the Domum. Keep your man fed, and he'll be happy. Back then I didn't realize part of the care and feeding of men was allowing them free reign of your body.

"I'm not hungry, Imogene." His eyes dart to the couch. "Sit."

I swallow and do as I'm told, sitting on the edge of the chair, eyes cast down. "Have I done something to upset you?"

His hand shoots out, fingers rough on my chin, and he lifts my gaze to his. "Fuck no, Little Lamb. It's not you I'm angry with, it's..." His whole body stiffens further. "Elon told me what happened on the delivery—how you could have been hurt." His touch lightens, fingers trailing down my neck. "I'm furious at my father for allowing this to go so far." The hand by his side clenches tight. "I'm furious that anyone would think they could have you without my permission."

"It was okay," I say, taking that fist into my hands and loosening his fingers. "Elon was there. He protected me."

His blue eyes meet mine. "It's *my* job to protect you."

"Apparently, it requires more than one man to keep me safe." I smile up at him. "I'm just thankful you allow the others to be there, too."

"You like them, don't you?"

"They're growing on me," I admit. "Even Elon."

"I'm glad. I know it's unconventional, even in Serendee, to belong to more than one mate, but you're right. To protect you, to keep you safe, to keep you ours, it has to be all of us."

We sit like this for a long beat, me holding his hand, him grazing his fingertips along the column of my neck. My heart flutters, the fear having vanished. Having this man's attention—in a good way—is almost more than I can handle. His eyes dart down to my mouth, and he tilts his head, drawing me in for a kiss.

For once he's not angry or punishing—there's no manipulation, and I sink into him, the warmth of his tongue and the feel of his strong jaw. My body buzzes, humming the strains of an invisible music, and God, this is what I've been wanting from this man. This kind of tenderness and care.

Apparently, all it took was my life being threatened to bring him to surface.

His hand drops to the buttons at my neckline, working each one out of its hole. It's painfully tedious, my heart threatening to rip from my chest. I barely hear the front door open and close, although I'm aware of Elon the moment he walks in.

His presence is undeniable.

"Go away," Rex says, also aware of his friend standing five feet away. He never stops unbuttoning my dress.

"Rex," Elon says.

He kisses me, deep and long before pulling back to say, "Fuck off. Whatever it is, it can wait."

His casual but determined banter catches me off guard. Does he want me that much? My body warms and I catch the way his lips quirk, coy and sexy. I can't help but smile back.

Elon, determined as ever, doesn't leave. "We have a job."

Rex sighs and gives me a look that says, '*don't move,*' and stands up. "Fuck the job. I need some time with my mate."

Elon's eyes meet mine, and I see a dark urgency behind them. As much as I want Rex, this sweet, protective mate to stay at home with me, I squeeze his hand and say, "Go with him. He wouldn't come in here if it wasn't important."

The two men stare at one another for a long moment, but I know that Elon's going to win when Rex runs a hand through his hair and grunts, "Fine." He turns to me, grabbing my hand and lifting me from the couch. His hands circle my waist. "We're not done, Little Lamb."

I nod and push up on my toes, kissing him on the jaw. His face turns and his lips meet mine, drawing me in for another kiss.

"Be careful," I say as his hand eases off my hip. I'm spurred to go to Elon. He watches me closely as I take his hand. "You, too. Don't do anything dangerous."

He brushes the hair off my cheek and skims his fingers down the side of my face, to my chin. He tilts it up and kisses me. Like everything else about him, it's hard and full of deep intensity. When he pulls away, I feel wobbly on my feet.

Rex gets his jacket and I notice as he shrugs it on there's a black gun nestled against the small of his back. He lifts his chin. "Tell Levi and Silas we'll be back as soon as possible."

Feeling a chill from seeing the gun, I wrap my arms around my upper body, seeking warmth or assurance. An anxious feeling builds inside of me, and I'm aware that it's not new, that it's been growing for days.

Things are about to change and I'm not sure if I'm ready.

WHEN I HEAR a sound at the door, I think it's Levi or Silas returning home for the night. Neither man emerges and then I realize it's a knock—soft—barely a tap. I push back the curtain on the window and see a young boy—maybe eight or nine.

"Hello," I say, opening the door.

"Are you Imogene?"

"Yes."

He holds out a square envelope—my name scrawled across the front. "This is for you."

I recognize the script—it's the same as the ones to all the other women's meetings—and it sets my heart racing. While looking over his shoulder, making sure no one sees me, I take it from him.

"Thank you."

He nods, and jumps down the porch steps, vanishing down the road. I don't go back inside before I run a finger under the flap and open it. More instructions. The meeting is tonight. Eleven PM. Dress in ceremonial white.

There's a tug at my heart this time—less excitement—more worry. Rex and I were on the precipice of something. A more honest, real relationship. I know him well enough now, that if he finds out that I've been attending this women's group, becoming more bonded to the women in Serendee, he'll be furious.

Betrayed.

Things are changing so quickly for me. It's confusing and over-whelming. Rex and the guys have shown me this other side of life: sex, lust, and every temptation in the outside world. The information about my mother and Beatrice. The Fallen. But then the women's group... it's the kind of acceptance I've always wanted in the community.

It's an honor I never expected to receive.

Being part of this bonded group of women is important to me, but I also feel like I'm losing another piece of myself with each meeting. Telling Margaret about sleeping with men other than my mate, well, it's all twisted and confusing.

Regardless of my mixed feelings, there's no real way I can decline the invitation. I've already committed. I've given them my collateral. I've taken the oaths.

As always, I do as I'm instructed, changing into my white dress, slipping on my sandals. Like a ghost, I slip into the night, traveling up the hill to the meeting spot—Beatrice' house. Margaret is waiting with a wide, welcoming smile.

"Sorry it was so last minute," she says. "Did you make it out okay."

"Rex and Elon were called away to an assignment. Silas and Levi didn't make it home."

"Good. I set it up for them to not be home, but juggling four men is a challenge."

I laugh and say, "Tell me about it," even though the knowledge that she orchestrated their assignments fills my belly with worry. This woman has so much power.

"Tonight is going to be so special, Imogene." She thrusts both hands out, fingers wiggling for me to grasp. "But before we go, there's something I want to share with you—since we're family."

"Oh," I say, "is something wrong?"

"No, the opposite really." She pulls my hand to her stomach. The move startles me, but not as much as the feel of a bump under the loose, flowing dress. *A bump.* I blink and look at her face. She's beaming. "I'm pregnant."

The news hits me—hard like an impact. Shock? Surprise. Maybe both.

"Rex is going to be a big brother and you're going to be a sister-in-law." She laughs, possibly knowing how crazy it sounds. Or, hopefully she does. He'll be over twenty years older than the baby.

"I'm just..." I suck in a breath. "Congratulations. That's amazing news."

"Isn't it?" She looks down, rubbing her hand over the swell of her stomach. She looks to be a few months—although Margaret is so thin, she may be further along. "It just makes tonight even more special."

I tilt my head to the side. "How so?"

"Tonight is when we truly become sisters." She squeezes my hand. "Now that you've released your collateral and have committed to the women's group, there's one last step." She lowers her voice. "Tonight, in a special ceremony, you'll get your birthmark."

The birthmark. She'd told us about this the first night in the woods. The final step of our initiation. I shiver, unable to discern if it's nerves or excitement. No, what Anex would tell me is that it's fear. Fear of embracing Enlightenment. Fear of handing myself over to a trusted spiritual leader.

I squeeze Margaret's fingers in mine and say with complete honesty, "I can't wait."

23

E^{lon}

I SHIFT the car into gear, pushing the speed limit, as we exit the county. The road is familiar. I'd driven it two days before. This time I know what I'm getting into.

"Is someone going to tell me where we're going?" Silas asks from the back seat. I'd picked him up on the way to the garage, telling him we needed him. Which we didn't. Not for the easy drop off over at the Phi Kappa house.

It was the second, unofficial job I had planned. One I detailed to Rex after we left Imogene at the house. Our kind of work isn't exactly in Silas' wheelhouse, but he can use a gun. Every male in Serendee knows how to wield a weapon and defend the community. It's a concept ingrained in us since childhood. If shit goes sideways tonight, and it may, I want backup.

"Anex has communicated to some of the people we do business

with, that members of our community are for sale," I say. "We're going to send a message that not everyone in Serendee agrees."

"Especially," Rex says, inspecting one of the guns he brought with him. The silver metal glints in a passing headlight, "When they're trying to buy my mate."

"Say that again?" Silas says, moving into the gap between the seats.

"I went on a sales trip yesterday, trying to fix a prior delivery error," I say, catching his eye in the mirror. His expression is hard, eyes tense. We're used to bending to the rules of our home—to our leader—but this is one step too far. "My apology and money weren't enough. The bastard wanted Imogene as part of the deal."

"Son of a bitch," Silas swears. "And let me guess... the people Anex has for sale are the Fallen."

It's not a question. "Yep."

"Fuck," he says, followed by a string of curse words. "I knew something was off."

I agree. The way those women looked in those tiny, filthy cells... it's been gnawing at me for days. One moment those people were productive members of the community. The next they'd crossed Anex in some unforgivable way, and their lives were over.

"My father just keeps pushing and pushing the boundaries of what our community is supposed to be about. Weapons, drugs, re-education, and now sex trafficking? This is way outside of the foundation of Serendee."

I know it's hard for Rex to admit it. Even if he's harbored suspicions about his mother's death, and dislikes his father, he's spent years reaping the rewards of Anex's control and command of the community, but he's right. We can't allow this to continue.

Risking Imogene's safety was the final straw.

"So what's the plan?" Silas asks, as I turn off the highway and down a long, dark road.

"We're going to give Jeb a little visit." I ground my jaw. "That bastard almost killed me."

I explain to them both exactly what went down, how Jeb and

his wife pulled guns and are fighters. "They're extremists of some kind," I add. "Living off the grid, dealing to backwoods communities, heavily armed..."

"So you mean like Serendee?" Rex asks, the sarcasm thick.

If it didn't rankle every belief, every foundation of my entire identity I'd agree, but it does, so I don't.

"That's it," I say, instead, gesturing to the little shack by the road. "His file noted that they live in a house at the back of the property."

Anex keeps dossiers on everyone we work with, from frat boys to isolated extremists.

"Jesus," Silas mutters, eyeing the run-down stand. "I fucking hate hillbillies."

"Anyone else lives with them?" Rex asks.

"Just the wife as far as I know." I didn't see any other occupants in the house, but with a guy like Jeb, you never know.

We park down at the end of the road, car tucked in near the farm stand, checking weapons and securing them before we head down the long driveway. Sure enough, there's a small house up ahead, lights warming the windows in an otherwise pitch black night. It's quiet and Silas picks up a rock, tossing it toward the house, trying to rouse a dog or anyone else watching. When no one responds, I nod to Rex to take the back door. He vanishes around the side, a stick snapping under his foot. I hold my breath, waiting for all hell to break loose, but the same stillness fills the night air. When Silas finally exhales next to me, I realize he is, too.

"*On three*," I mouth, holding my gun at level. I count down and rear back, kicking my foot into the door. It splinters in a loud slap, voices shouting from the interior. We move so fast that the scream Jeb's wife is about to let loose is caught in her throat.

"Don't you dare," I tell her, pointing the gun at her. Jeb has his hand under the couch, and I see the black steel at his fingertips. "Touch that weapon and I'll blow her head off, Jeb." I jerk my chin at Silas, who is a foot behind Jeb with his gun cocked and ready. "And then he'll blow yours off, too."

Unbelievably, I can tell he's considering it, unphased by his wife's panicked whimpers. Finally, he relents, drawing his hand back. I bend and remove the shot gun, positioning it behind me.

"There," Jeb says, once he's lost his weapon. "I don't know what the fuck you're doing on my property like this, but I can tell you that you've lost your goddamn mind." His eyes narrow. "Your guru knows you're here?"

"He's not a guru," I reply, not even sure what that word means. "He made an error and we're here to rectify it."

"By what? Killing me and the wife? That's not rectifying anything—that's triggering a war." He grins, revealing crooked and yellow teeth. "Once Anex's buyers find out about this, everything he's built up will crash."

"You think you're that important?" Silas asks, hand shaking. He's still furious that this man tried to take Imogene. I can see the darkness in his eyes. "You're nothing."

"I may live out here alone, minding my own business, son, but your leader is a dangerous man. There are protocols put in place in case he," he glances at me, "or his minions, decide to overstep." He laughs. "You kill me and a tremor will travel across Anex's enterprises, and you'll be the one to feel the aftershocks."

I lunge, grabbing him by the shirt, and lifting him off the couch. My nose is less than an inch from his when I hear the trigger cock. Somehow, somewhere he had another gun and I feel the hard press in my gut.

The two of us are in a stand-off, my gun pressed against his throat. His to my gut. Silas covers the wife and fuck it all, we're screwed.

"You may want to lower the gun." Rex's voice amplifies the tension. My eyes are locked with Jeb's, and he doesn't take his eyes off me, but a panicked whimper from his wife forces me to break contact. Rex is standing at the entrance to the hallway, a young teenage girl in his grip. Sweat drips down my back. Fuck, shit just got worse, way worse.

"Jeb," the woman cries.

"Not now, Doreen," he snaps.

"Daddy?"

That's when it clicks—the pieces falling into place for Jeb. He turns, and the distraction is all I need to grab the pistol, turning it back on him with sweaty hands.

Rex grins at the man, smile wide and evil. "The woman you tried to purchase yesterday is my mate," he growls. "How about I take your daughter back to Serendee with me, sell her to the highest bidder.

The girl shakes her head, fat tears running down her cheeks. I want to feel bad for her, but her father needs a lesson. *And* we need to get out of here alive.

"I thought we were making a deal," Jeb says, voice less sure. "You owed me."

"Bullshit," Rex strides forward, dragging the girl with him. "You wanted my woman. You wanted to put your filthy hands on her." He pushes the girl toward Silas who catches her, holding onto her tight. Rex grabs Jeb's arm and drags him over to the fireplace, pushing him to his knees and slamming his forearm against the stone surface. "You wanted to *use* her."

Seamlessly, Rex, pulls a knife out of his boot. Doreen and the daughter scream.

"Don't hurt him," the girl cries, turning her face into Silas' chest. As angry as he is, I see his hand curl around her shoulder. It's just his nature to provide comfort even while he has a gun to her temple.

Rex ignores her pleas and presses down on his wrist. "Maybe if you don't know how to keep your fucking hands to yourself, I should just remove the temptation. "

"No! Please! Don't! I didn't know she belonged to you! I thought that's why you brought her!"

Rex, lays the blade of the knife across Jeb's wrist, pressing gently. One move and I know he's got the strength to cut his hand clean off. I'm only a few feet away but I can barely hear him command, "Tell me everything."

"I-I got a message." Jeb's body trembles, head to toe. "Word about a new product. Women mostly, but a few boys if that's what's desired. Cash only. I seriously thought that since there was the product screw up, you'd brought me a bonus." He lifts his gaze to me. "No one has ever brought a woman to a drop before. Especially not one that looked like her."

The statement stings and the accusation is clear. I'm the one that put her in danger. He's not wrong.

"Let me make something clear," Rex says. "The people of Serendee are not for sale."

"You may want to tell your Daddy that, but between us, it's understood."

"That's not all," Rex says, pressing down. Blood beads and drips down his wrist. "Since you're so fucking connected, you notify everyone you know that we do not sell people." Jeb nods, but Rex continues. "If someone, including my father, tries to traffic any member of our community, or any other community, I'll hold you personally responsible."

"Yes. I understand," Jeb says, eyes pleading. Rex doesn't move, considering Jeb's commitment, but finally releases him. I nod at Silas, and he lets the girl go, too. She runs to her mother, folding into her side.

"This ends today," Rex says. "Your relationship with Serendee is over. Find another distributor." He looks over at Doreen and the girl. "And learn to treat women better. They aren't objects or possessions to buy and sell."

Those words haunt me as we leave, striding away in the dark, worming their way into my brain.

Serendee does sell people. Maybe not for money but good behavior. Loyalty. Devotion. Service. Girls are separated and trained. Arranged with a mate. There's no other option. It's all at Anex's choosing. And with Imogene? The four of us came along and made her our possession.

Fuck.

"We're going to pay for that," Silas says from the backseat. More than anyone he understands the consequences for defiant behavior. "He's going to find out and when he hears you cut him off as a buyer..."

There's no need to say anything else. We all know.

Ahead I see a junction, the split in the highway. One leads back to Serendee. The other to a little town I've never visited, but the address is stamped in my brain. Memorized just in case.

I take the unfamiliar road.

"Where are you going?" Rex asks.

"Silas is right, there will be consequences, but we're not going to be the one to suffer it."

"Shit," Silas says from the back seat. "Imogene."

I nod. "We're going to make sure that she's safe, even if that means letting her go."

24

L^{evi}

"JUST REMEMBER," I tell the class, "you are called to lead for a reason. You were born with the temperament to handle things the females in your life can't."

A hand raises in the back—Kenneth. Born and raised in Serendee. He's on the fast track with Anex and that's why he was invited to my class. I nod for him to ask his question.

He fidgets, shifting nervously in his seat. I raise an eyebrow and say, "This is a safe place to express yourself, Ken. Nothing said here, leaves here, right guys?"

The small group concurs, eager to help a fellow member.

He takes a breath. "What happens if your mate questions your authority. Calls you sexist or demeaning?"

"Ah," I say, ignoring the pink ruddiness on his cheeks. "I get it. Describing your flaws to the group is hard. Not being in control of your household is humiliating, but that's why we're here. To learn from one another." I sit on the stool in the font of the classroom. A method I learned from Anex about presenting myself as understanding and compassionate. "Taking care of you family isn't sexist. It's not demeaning. It's empowering. The Way shows us that time and time again, we revert to these roles, when we embrace our masculinity—and our positions of authority, the women in our lives feel safer. More secure." I grin. "More intimate and loving."

There's a chuckle at my insinuation. I mean, what do I know about love and mates? Yet Anex said The Way was calling me to teach this men's group. At least now I can draw on my experiences with Imogene.

She's not my mate and God knows if I love her—but there's something intense transpiring between us—something I can't describe, but I try to use that now to educate the men in the group.

"Part of my role in Serendee is to guide and implement Correction. Currently I have one female that I am guiding through this process." I exhale. "It hasn't been easy, but what I've come to learn is that I give her what she needs—and sometimes that pushes me to my limits."

Like the night with the knife. We pushed that so far, the boundary line snapped.

"Is it uncomfortable sometimes? Yes. But no one said following this way of life, following The Way, would be a cakewalk. We are given these roles as a challenge to ourselves and to those we guide —in Corrections, in Bonding, in any part of our lives in Serendee."

"She doesn't hate you for it?" Jacob, another member asks.

"No," I reply. "Actually, now she comes to me—willingly—we even discuss how far things should go." I look at Kenneth. "Show your mate your control, don't just tell her. Be there for her. Help her though her Lapses. Those actions are what define us."

He nods, seeming a little more confident and I use that as the opportunity to wrap up the class.

"Make sure you complete the worksheets for our next meeting." I slide off the stool. "I'll see you all next week."

I straighten up while the men file out of the room, handing me their guide books on the way out. The building grows quiet. It's evening and I should be the only one left, but I hear movement in the hallway and look up. To my surprise Anex stands in the doorway.

"Good evening, Levi."

"Oh." I stop what I'm doing, resting the stack of books on top of the shelf, and bow, touching my forehead. "I didn't know anyone else was here."

"Just doing a little last-minute work," he says, entering the room. "Whenever we're in a building phase, I tend to have more to check of my list."

"The childcare center?" I ask. "I saw the construction the other day. Looks like it's coming along."

"Nicely," he agrees. "That's actually what I came here to talk to you about."

I frown. "The childcare center?"

"Well, not exactly," he says, walking over to the stool. He eases up and nods to a chair in the front row. "Take a seat, Levi."

I walk over to the chairs and sit. It's a strange vantage point, I'm used to being the one at the front of the class, but at the same time, Anex is my teacher. I should be honored he's taken the time to address me personally. "What is it you need me to do?"

"This is actually about Imogene."

"Imogene?" A flicker of worry fills my chest. "What about her?"

"My family is growing, Levi. Margaret is with child. Rex has brought Imogene into our lives. After years of only having a son, I now have a family." The declaration seems harsh—seeing as how we thought *we* were his family, but I understand. It's why I crave a mate of my own. "The Way has spoken to me about how to integrate Imogene into the future of our family. After much meditation and thought, I've decided to move her out of her position here, at the Center and to the Childcare facility once it opens."

"That sounds like a wonderful opportunity," I say. Working in the Center is an honor, but so will a position at his new project. Anex choses positions carefully. "I know she loves her work here, she's very devoted, but working on a new project... I can only imagine she'll be excited."

"Change is hard for women like Imogene. Her defiant streak runs hot, but yes, I think she'll come around to it." He looks down at me. "It's out of necessity. Some recent activities, mostly outside of Serendee, have made me reassess. As a member of my direct family, the risks are too high for her to be outside of the community."

I nod. "That makes sense to keep Rex's mate safe."

I notice the slight twitch in his eye when I say Rex's name. I press forward. "I'm ready for whatever task you need me to do. I'm glad to help her transition if necessary. She's taken to me as her Guide, and I think I will be able to—"

"You will no longer be in charge of Imogene's Corrections."

The news hits me hard—like my anchor has been lifted and I'm suddenly unmoored. "I—" I clear my throat, trying to compose myself. "Can I ask why?"

"As you just said, you've done remarkable work guiding Imogene during the transition of her Order. It was no easy feat, not with her temperament, and Rex's determination to muddy her mind about Serendee with his toxic beliefs." His voice is calm, collected, even though I know Rex's Regression bothers him deeply. "Tonight, she will complete her initiation with the women's group. Despite the distractions by my son, she has taken the steps toward higher Enlightenment. She's ready for more and I applaud you for your role in that—it's just no longer needed."

"Anex—if I may," I say, trying to soothe the panic building in my chest, "Imogene will still require Corrections. Like you said, she has a defiant streak and the only thing to keep her in line is by addressing her Lapses."

"I agree," he says, "which is why I, as the leading male in her family, will take over her Corrections."

"You?" I whisper.

"Of course. It's my duty." He looks over my head, around the room. "Is that what you've been teaching in your course?"

"I—" I swallow. "Yes."

He smiles, kind and empathetic. "Don't worry, I'm not demoting you or anything. With the growth of my family and obligations to Serendee, I will need you to take over some of my obligations." My back straightens. This is... a surprise. An honor. "I would like you to take over the re-education of the Fallen."

The Fallen. I'm aware of who they are, and where they live. They have not been part of my duties—but Silas'. He has told me about the women kept there and how just visiting drains him. I have seen Bethany with my own eyes as she serves us during our private meetings with Anex.

I know what re-education means. These people are the dregs of Serendee. No matter what he says, it's a demotion. Or at the very least a punishment. My mind races, what have I done to deserve this and then it hits me.

I'm too close to the one person he wants the most: Imogene.

I swallow the lump in my throat. "Thank you for the consideration," I say, "but I am not sure I'm comfortable with that position."

Anex's eyes narrow. "Are you trying to decline the opportunity I just offered you?"

"I think it would be of better use here—teaching this class. Instructing the men on how to manage themselves and their households." I'm aware that what I am doing is unheard of—saying no to Anex. I have never done it before. Not once. But he's just taken the one thing I've ever wanted—ever had—away from me and now... he's giving me the rejects? The worst of our kind? "I'm sorry, I just don't think that this is the best use of my skills and gifts given to me by The Way."

He stares at me, unmoving, for a long moment. Enough time for sweat to bead on the back of my neck. Finally, he slides off the stool and says, "I understand."

I rise from my seat. "I'm sorry."

"No, don't be." He steps forward, thrusting out his hand. I give him mine and he clasps them together. "You've always been my most devoted son," he says. "If you feel called to decline this opportunity, then I must consider that."

I exhale. "Thank you."

He cups my cheek with his hand. "Thank *you* for your honestly, Levi. I wish more of the people close to me were."

The smile he gives me before he walks out of the room doesn't quite reach his eyes and it fills me with an uneasiness. It could be from the shock of everything I just learned.

One thing I know for certain, things are changing in Serendee and I suspect it's going to impact us all.

25

I mogene

I'M BLINDFOLDED AGAIN and forced to trust Margaret as she guides me through Serendee in the dark. She's careful, and although we take circular route, I can tell when we enter the main house. It has a certain scent—less earthy than the rest of the homes, where air conditioning units are frowned upon, and solar panels provide much of our energy.

I almost ask why we're going to Anex's home—Margaret had assured me this group was disconnected from him outside of his blessing and approval. Something about being here makes me feel uneasy. I can't help but think about the women in the cells below, the Fallen.

"You'll wait here," Margaret says, nudging me into a room. Her hand clamps down on my forearm and squeezes. "After tonight, I won't be just your Main but your sister, too."

I hear others. Their shifting feet and a few other sounds of anxiety. We shouldn't be afraid to have our vision blocked. We're Enlightened and our other senses should take over. At least that's what I remind myself once the door closes and Margret leaves, and my pulse starts to race.

"Keep your blindfolds on," a voice calls, breaking the quiet. "But remove your clothing."

"All of it?" a soft voice asks.

"Strip completely. Tonight isn't about material bindings. It's about spiritual ones. Connecting to the other women in the group. There's no reason to hide your true selves. Not your body, nor your mind, or your secrets."

Something nags at me as I obey, unbuttoning the tiny pearl buttons on the front of my dress. Maybe it's because for once I do belong to someone else—more than one person. We're in a relationship. Committed, even if by arrangement. My agreement with Rex is deeper than the one I made during the ceremonies. We've made promises to one another. My body belongs to him and the other men in our home. Something tells me he wouldn't like the fact I'm revealing myself to others.

Still, I do as I'm told. How can I not? My dress slips from my shoulders, and I remove my Serendee approved undergarments. Fabric rustles around me as the other women do the same.

Little Lamb.

The nickname echoes in my head, but it feels wrong. I'm not a lamb. I'm nothing more than a sheep.

"We're ready," that same voice says, light and full of joy. "Grab the hand of the person next to you and follow me."

I'm trying to reconcile my thoughts, my emotions, the thrumming in my chest, when a hand grabs mine and pulls, dragging me along with the others. My steps are clumsy, and our bare bodies run into one another. Nervous laughter bubbles from somewhere ahead. I sense when we cross the threshold. It's the scent that hits me. The smell of antiseptic. The blast of cold, sterile air. My nipples, already hard, tighten painfully. Goosebumps spread across my flesh. The pit of my stomach clenches, turning over. And I know before our host says, "You can remove your blindfolds," exactly where we are.

The healer's room.

Anex's healer's room.

I peel back the blindfold and see that I'm one of four other women. There had been more initially. Had they not made it to this part of the process? That thought sends a jolt of pride to my chest, but it's tempered when I look away from the other women and take in the room—I've been here before. The medical table in the middle of the room, where I was studied and tested, twice on the command of our leader. The table is covered in a white sheet, the symbol of innocence and purity, but that weird, distressed feeling in my belly only intensifies.

Margaret, in a white cloak, steps forward, a serene smile on her mouth.

"Welcome," she says, spreading her arms. "This is the night you've been waiting for. You've completed your steps. Your commitment to the women in Serendee. You've given your collateral and been deemed worthy. Anex has given me full control over this group and through that power, I am able to tell you that you've been chosen for the final step that will make us sisters."

Her words set me on edge. I'm reminded of the fallen, the girl babbling about the sacrifices she was making to attain Anex's approval. Are Margaret's words any different?

"Tonight you'll take the mark of our group—a birthmark. This is a rebirth. One not tied to your parents or anyone else. You'll be tied to Serendee. To The Way." She makes a symbol with her fingers, that looks like a sideways 'W.' "We're women. We're Enlightened."

Those words send a shiver down my spine. Enlightened? That's the ultimate goal. And this ceremony is the final step? There's an immediate shift in the nervous energy that filled the room when we walked in. Now it's anticipation. Our nudity and sacrifice make sense: we must shed everything to reach this state. Our fears. Our pride. Our modesty.

We've been chosen.

"Let me prepare you," Margaret adds, "this won't be easy. It will hurt, but from pain comes empowerment. And if you violate the sanctity of your sisterhood, your collateral will be exposed to your loved ones, your community, and Anex." She taps on the door, and it opens, another woman in white joining us. "Healer Bloom has been anointed to assist in the process. I'm grateful for her strength and skills."

The woman crosses the room and stops at a rolling cart arranged with instruments. A square box fills most of the space. She rolls it over to the exam table and presses several buttons before lifting something that looks like a wand.

"Kayla." Margaret nods to the woman next to me. "You're first."

Kayla steps forward and Margaret meets her, pulling her into a hug. She whispers something in her ear and gives her a hand as she climbs onto the table.

"We'll need your assistance," Margaret says. "Come hold your sister through her experience. She may fight due to the intensity, but remember, she chose to be here, she was *chosen* to be here. Help her get through to the other side."

The three other women and I surround Kayla, two by her arms and two by her legs. I am at her upper body, where I can see her face. I smile down at her, hoping to be reassuring, but all I feel is my own anxiety. "You're strong," I tell her. "Worthy."

"I'm scared of needles," she whispers, assuming the mark is a tattoo.

"Face that fear. Own it."

She nods and adds, "Thank you."

Margaret lays a square of paper on the flesh below her hip and dabs a cloth on top. When she pulls the paper back, the symbol is there. A sideways 'W' with a small slash over the left side. It's elegant with thin lines. My fears dissipate, knowing I'll be carrying something with such meaning on my person.

Kayla watches as Healer Bloom holds up the wand, the metal

tip, shining in the overhead light. Holding it like a pencil, she lowers it to the template and presses down.

I expect a buzz, the sound of needles inking the skin, but the room fills with Kayla's screams. In the chaos, Margaret is louder.

"Hold her down! Hold her down! Don't let her move! It's for the greater good! It's the pain that leads to empowerment!"

My eyes flick to the woman across from me. Her name is Dorothy. I don't know her well other than she's a few years older than me and works at the farm. Her eyes well with tears but she never falters, holding onto Kayla's arm with all her strength.

I look down at the woman I know Silas' recruited into the community. She chose to be here, to leave her family and join this way of life. It's harder, I think, than growing up in Serendee. But now as she fights to sit up our eyes meet, hers are pleading. Filled with betrayal.

A fleeting thought runs through my head.

What would my mother do?

As if reading my mind, Margaret shouts, "If you allow your sister to fail, you all fail." Her eyes meet mine. "You don't want to fail. I can promise you that."

In the heat of the room, the sweat and panic, naked and fearful, I look down at Kayla and say, "I'm sorry," and tighten my grip. Someone shoves a strap in her mouth, her teeth bearing down on the leather. A moment later the room is filled with the scent of burning flesh.

Kayla never stops looking at me and I see the hate. It's deep in the green of her eyes, or maybe it's just my reflection. Either one I know I'm no one's sister.

I'm just a sheep.

THE SUN RISES to the east on our return home. The ceremony took hours, and after the screams the quiet of the streets only amplifies the numb sensation overtaking my brain and body. The only exception is my lower hip, where the pain is searing. God, it hurts. Deep and painful, like they branded me all the way to the bone.

"I know that was a lot," Margaret says, keeping close. We were each escorted out of the mansion, sweaty and exhausted. She rests a hand on her belly, as if she's comforting the fetus inside. "But doesn't it feel amazing now?"

I want to tell her it hurts like hell, and not in the good way. I feel sick. Confused. Betrayed. I'm no innocent to pain, but this... it was otherworldly. No one screamed after Kayla. They didn't have the opportunity. Healer Bloom made sure the strap was placed in all our mouths before she started.

I still taste the leather on my tongue, the burnt skin in my nostrils, Kayla's screams in my ears.

"Imogene?" she prompts, forcing me to a stop.

My house is a few feet away. Lights blazing in the windows. They'll be waiting for me. I know it and I have no idea what I'm going to say about what's been done to me. What I allowed to be done.

"I'm fine," I lie. "Just tired. Like you said, it was overwhelming."

"You're special," Margaret says, pulling me into a hug. I fight a hiss when her lower body brushes against the wound on my hip. "More than the other women. You were chosen for a reason, don't forget that."

A month ago, those words would have given me a sense of validation, but now, I can't escape the uneasiness coursing through my veins. I give her a tight smile, hoping it comes off as exhaustion and tell her goodnight.

I step into the house, into the bright light of the foyer. I'm not surprised when Levi meets me there a moment later. "Where have you been?" he asks, rubbing at the heavy bags under his eyes. It's obvious he hasn't slept.

"A meeting," is all I get out before he strides toward me, grabbing my hand and pushing up my sleeve. A dark bruise mottles the skin from where I'd been restrained.

"What kind of meeting?" His voice is low. Dangerous. "Who did this to you?"

I don't get the chance to answer before the door opens and heavy footsteps enter the house. Levi's eyes dart over my shoulder and I turn. Rex, Elon and Silas appear, looking as worn out as I feel.

"What's going on?" Silas asks, taking us in.

"I just got home. There was a..." I search for an excuse but simply say. "I met some of the other women." I swallow. "Margaret invited me."

A flicker passes through Levi's eyes. Something I can't discern. "Is that where you got the bruises from?"

"What bruises?" Rex asks, closing the space between us. His picks up my other hand and reveals the marks on the other arm. He swears when he sees them.

"Were you restrained?" he asks. His voice takes on that tone— the one I can't quite identify. Anger? Distrust? Suspicion?

I pull my hand away, but in the process hit my hip. I yelp and soon all four of them are on me. "You're hurt," Silas says, eyes meeting mine. "Where?"

Elon reaches for the hem of my dress. I try to step away but land against the hard muscle of Rex's stomach and chest. He holds onto me, while Elon lifts the fabric up, looking for whatever caused my pain.

"I'm fine," I tell them, but tears well in my eyes from the burn. From the betrayal. I know what I've done is wrong. Even if it's unspoken, the branding is a violation to my commitment to Rex. I can feel it. I know it.

Elon lifts my dress until he spots the bandaged wound. Silas steps forward and slowly removes the tape, revealing the branding.

"Christ," Elon mutters. "What the hell is that?"

Rex leans over my shoulder, trying to get a better look. He must see it because he growls in my ear. "*Who* the hell did that to you?"

"I'm getting my kit," Silas says, staring at the wound long and hard before running down the hall.

A million questions run across Levi's expression as he stares at the brand, but he doesn't ask one of them. He just looks at the wound, like he can't figure out how it got there.

I shake my head so forcefully, tears fall. "I can't tell," I say to all of them, although Rex is the one that asked.

"Yes, you can, Imogene," he says. "You can and will."

"No," I try to pull away, but Elon's hand is clamped tight around my unbranded hip. "I can't. Not without endangering all of you."

Rex has grown eerily still and I turn, forcing myself to look at him. He's staring at the branding, head tilted, eyes slightly glazed. I wait for the rage, the accusation, but he shudders an exhale and says, "Fucking hell. Goddamn him."

Him.

"It wasn't your father," I say. Silas returns, his kit already open and he eases me away from Rex and Elon, down on the couch. Levi takes the seat next to me and together they sort through his salves and creams.

"No?" Rex asks, unphased by the men caring for me. "Who else would brand my father's initials in your skin?"

"It's not his initials. There's no 'A.'"

He reaches out, finger pointed. I brace myself for the pain of his touch, but he simply traces in the air. "T. W—Timothy Wray. My father had someone brand you with his fucking initials."

I look down, past the image I'd been told was being branded on me. The 'E' for Empowerment and Enlightenment. A sideways 'W' for Women and The Way. And see it for what it really is.

Anex branded me and four other women with his initials, like we were nothing but livestock down in the barn.

The rush of bile rises in the back of my throat, and I hold onto my stomach, trying to keep it down. Levi looks stricken by the knowledge and Elon storms out of the room. A moment later, something big and breakable crashes against the floor, followed by the sound of fists slamming into the plaster.

"Rex," I say, wanting to explain, but, how can I? The collateral. The threats. And now this? Anex must have been behind it the whole time. This was no exclusive group. It was another manipulation. Another level of control.

I walked straight into it like a lamb to slaughter.

I look to Rex and see his handsome face, twisted into furious rage. "Who was it?! Who the fuck branded my father's initials into your skin? Margaret?"

"If I tell—"

"I don't give a shit what they threatened you with, Imogene. There is nothing my father can do to me, Elon, Silas, or Levi that justifies this." Our eyes lock. "Tell me."

"A-a while back I was invited to join a women's group. I was told it was exclusive to women—blessed by your father, but that he was not involved." Silas wipes the branding with a damp cloth, and I hiss at the pain. "Oh god... I thought it was just women—like the men's group. A way to Empower and work on our Indulgences in a safe space. The meetings felt sacred—special, because only a few other women were invited. Things were secretive and, yes, there were times I wasn't comfortable with what they wanted me to do. But isn't that what we're taught? Enlightenment is uncomfortable." Fresh tears build in my eyes. "By the time I realized what was happening, it was too late. I was committed."

"What did they want you to do?" Elon asks, he's returned, uncaring about the blood dripping from his knuckles.

"I had to give them collateral—something personal about myself that they could then reveal to the community if I broke any of the rules." I look at each of them. "Including telling you."

"What kind of collateral did you give them?" Rex asks.

"I didn't tell him about looking for your mother or mine. I didn't tell them anything about how much you hate this place or how you think Anex killed your mother, but," I stare down at the branding, wincing as Silas uses a Q-tip to apply salve, "I did tell them about us. I told them about our relationship—about how all of us—together. I had to write it down and hand it over."

Silas' movements stop. The other men grow still. I force myself to look at them.

"I had to say something, you understand that, right?"

Although Anex gave his approval for the men to train me for Rex, this is not something the rest of the community will find acceptable. Anex Orders us to another member of the community. We Bond. We Mate. If he denies that he requested me to do this, and I have no doubt he will, we will be shunned.

I've put us all at terrible risk all because I wanted to feel special —accepted.

"I had no idea it would go this far," Levi says, voice panicked. "When he told us about the group, I didn't know he would use it to manipulate it—"

"What did you say?" Rex asks.

Silas curses and stands. "Look, man. We knew about the women's group. Anex told us it was for Imogene's good."

"And you just went along with it?" Rex asks. His eyes dart to Elon. "You knew about this?"

"Yes, but—"

Rex slams his hand in the air, palm out, shutting him off. "You hid this from me? All of you? About my mate? When you know my father had had nefarious intentions toward her the whole time?"

"What are we supposed to do? We have no other choice. This is our home. Our livelihood." Elon's voice cracks. He sounds scared. Something I've never heard from him before. "He's our leader."

Rex stills in the middle of the room, hands shoved in his pockets. The dark smudges under his eyes look more pronounced. He's exhausted, like we all are. No one is thinking clearly. We're all in pain.

"Can we just —" I start, hoping we can sleep on it and think clearly in the morning, but Rex straightens his shoulders and waves me off.

"I can't do this anymore," he says, "I cannot allow him to control my life. Not anymore." He walks down the hallway and out the front door, slamming it behind him. The four of us sit in silence, before Elon turns to go after him.

"Wait." Levi stands. "Let me go."

When the two look at one another, something passes between them. Elon nods, stepping aside to allow Levi to pass him in the hallway. It's in that moment that Elon stops and grabs him by the forearm. "Don't let him do anything stupid."

"I won't." Levi glances back, eye locking with mine. "I'll get him back."

The door closes softer this time and I exhale, staring down at the branding, the T and the W so obvious now.

Everything seems obvious.

Except for the way out.

26

L^{evi}

THE STREET IS empty when I get out to the porch, and I scan both directions. At the end of the street, I see a shadowy figure slip around the corner. It's the way to the Main House.

Jumping down the steps, I race after him, quickly getting to the corner. It's morning and a few people are up, headed to the farm or other early-day jobs.

"Morning," I say to one of the men I know works at the dairy barn. He tips his hat in greeting but I sense the judgment in his eyes as they skim over my rumpled clothes and unshaven face.

I don't owe that man any explanation. I'm one of the Chosen. Our ways aren't questioned the same way it would be if the roles were reversed.

"Rex," I call, jogging after him. "Hold up."

He doesn't stop, in fact, I'm pretty sure he widens his stride. He may be bigger than I am, but I'm fit, and I jog to catch up. When I finally fall into step, I realize that, like me, in the light of day, he looks rough.

"Listen, we shouldn't have kept the information about the women's meeting from you."

His eyes cut my way. "No, you shouldn't have."

"We don't have the ability to rebel against Anex the way you do. He's our leader—"

"Jesus." He stops, running his hand through his hair. "I'm tired of the excuses. He told you do to something. To lie to me, and all three of you fell into line. I get it," he says, "your loyalty is to him, not me."

"It's not that—"

But it is and we both know it. Anex has us by the balls. Our livelihoods, our shelter, food, clothing, *everything* is controlled by that man. Rex stares at me. "That's not the problem, Levi."

"Then what is?"

"You knew, and you didn't keep her safe."

That one lands—harder than a punch—because he's right.

"I'm sorry."

His jaw sets. "I'm not the one you should apologize to." He sets off again, striding up the hill, the big white house looming on the hill.

I follow, keeping up with his long legs. "It'll just get worse if you confront him."

"I'm not going to Anex," he says, still walking.

"Then what are you doing?"

He spins, stopping a few feet up the hill from me. "To get money. Supplies. A vehicle. I've got it all stashed for the right time."

"You're running?"

It wouldn't be the first time he's threatened it.

"I'm not running," he says, voice tight, "I'm getting her the fuck out of here. For good."

Imogene. He wants to save her.

. . .

I'M at a loss for words, but he's not finished. "My father's business is out of control. He's stepping into dangerous territory, and I don't want to be here when it implodes. I also don't want him to have any reason to use my mate as leverage. That branding was about ownership. Control. He put it there because, like the cows down at the barn, he views her as his property. *His.* Not mine." His eyes hold mine. "Not *ours.*"

"Where will you take her?" I ask. "Because he'll find you. He'll send his men out to bring her back."

Rex's expression changes, to something wary and worn. His arms cross over his chest and, even though he's my friend, I understand it's meant to be intimidating. "If I tell you, can I trust you not to take this back to my father?"

It's a fair question. Of all of us, my loyalty to Anex is the strongest, but things have shifted since Imogene came into our lives. Rex is right. His father branded her for a reason. A visible, painful reminder of who she belongs to.

The pieces of my conversation with him at the Center fall into place. He told me that tonight was a big deal. He's changing her job, taking over her Corrections.

God, Rex needs to get her out of here *now.*

"I won't tell him anything, I promise."

The look he gives me is skeptical.

I dig my nails into the wood of the fence. "You're right. I haven't been protecting her. Not the way I should. I will not risk hurting her even more by telling your father any of this." I lift my chin. "I stood up to him tonight. He asked me to do something and I said no."

Rex's eyebrows raise. "How did that go?"

"I don't know."

But deep down I know I fucked up. Big. "If you tell me what your plan is, I can help you."

Our friendship runs deep. Different from him and Elon, who have bonded over their jobs outside this world, or with Silas with who he shares the guiltiest of pleasures. But we've always been friends—tight—and I hope he can still trust me.

"My plan is to take her to someone who is willing to fight for her more than anyone else." His eyes dart around. "Her mother."

My chest tightens. This is real. He's not fucking around this time. Panic burns. "You found her?"

"Yes. Well, Elon found her. But tonight, after we handled the Jeb situation, we went to locate her."

Blood rushes to my ears as I listen to my friend describe what happened that night. Rex, Elon, and Silas went to the address they found on the internet. It's a meeting space, for people that have escaped a cult or for family members wanting to help their family and loved ones out of a cult.

"She was there," he says, 'closing up after a meeting."

"And?"

"She recognized me," he admits. "I look a lot like my father did at my age—when they were friends. It took me a few minutes—mostly Silas—to convince her we weren't there for trouble, but to talk to her about Imogene."

I grab ahold of the picket fence just off the side of the road, bracing myself.

"And?"

"And she wants her. She's always wanted her. My father was the obstacle in the way."

A wave of emotion rolls over me. Panic. Curiosity. Fear. When it settles, one bubbles to the surface: Anger. "So what? You pack her up and just drop her off at her mother's house? To a woman she hasn't seen in years? Stealing her from the only home she's known her entire life and tossing her into the secular world?"

"I want to get her somewhere safe, Levi, and this is my only option."

"There's nowhere safer than Serendee."

"Do you really believe that? After seeing that brand on her? After seeing the marks you've given her?"

It's a low blow, but one I maybe deserve. Still, I deflect. "She asks for the Corrections, Rex, begs for Enlightenment."

"Why?" Rex's voice trembles. "Why do you think she wants you to Correct her like that?"

When I don't answer he turns away, but I hear him clearly when he says, "She's as bad as The Fallen. As compliant and confused, you know that right? For every effort I made to break that out of her, it was pointless. Imogene is *already* broken. I don't know if there's a way to fix her."

"So that's what this is about? You're throwing her away? Tossing her aside like a broken toy?" The rage builds in my chest. "Angry because your father marked her first?

"Shut up," Rex says, arms dropping to his sides, while his chest puffs out.

"No, because someone has to talk some sense into you." My voice rises and I'm aware of a couple walking within earshot. I lower it. "He will find you, and when he does, it will be a hundred times worse."

"Maybe that's just what he wants us to think." His chest rises and falls, like he's barely containing his own anger. "She needs to get away from the darkness of this place. I've spent most of my life being a selfish prick, Levi. For once, just let me do the right thing."

His eyebrows raise, like he's offering me the chance to challenge him one last time. I don't. He's right. We may not be able to save ourselves, but we can do the right thing for her.

"Go," I tell him. "Get everything ready and let me know what you need me to do."

"Thank you," he says, thrusting out his hand.

I look at it, prepared to shake it, but instead step forward, dragging him into a hug. "Just make sure she's safe," I say. "For real safe."

"You got it, brother."

We separate, and as he walks toward the house, I don't know why it feels like a goodbye. Maybe it's just the reality of what comes next, or the sensation of separating the past and the future. No matter what it is, whatever comes next will change life for all of us.

I'VE JUST STEPPED into the house when the music starts.

Clair de Lune. The solemn strains rise from the speakers situated through the community. Serendee is being called to the community center by Anex.

Despite my complete exhaustion, I stop by the living room where I find everyone asleep. Elon has sprawled out on the couch. Silas is across from him in an armchair, his feet propped on the coffee table and Imogene is curled up on the love seat. I shake her awake first.

"Did you find him?" she asks, rubbing her eyes.

"Yes," I tilt my head. "But there's no time to talk about it now. We're being summoned."

Her eyes widen as the music processes and she nods, standing quickly. She winces at the pain blow her hip.

"You okay?" I ask, worried about the wound. It's deep and ugly.

"I'm fine," she says, reaching to smooth her hair. "We need to hurry."

I wake the others, jostling them from sleep. "Come on, there's a meeting."

Silas groans, rubbing his face while Elon stretches his arms over his head. I don't miss the lines of worry on his forehead when he asks, "Is this about Rex?"

"I don't see how, I just left him a few minutes ago and he wasn't going to see his father."

Elon and Silas exchange a look, both skeptical. I don't blame them, but I feel confidant Rex was telling me the truth.

"I guess we'll find out soon enough," Silas says, slipping on his shoes. The music grows louder—that's what happens. It starts off low and gentle, but then grows with volume and aggression as the minutes pass.

The four of us quickly get to the community center, funneling in with the rest of the residents. It takes longer during the day with people scattered all over Serendee and in town. As usual,

Anex's chair is positioned in the middle of the stage—what's different is the lack of other seats—the ones for the inner circle. Our seats.

They've been removed.

"What the..." Elon mutters. Imogene tugs his hand and pulls him over where there's an empty section on the floor.

"Weird," Silas says, still a little groggy, but not enough to miss the strange vibe in the room. "Do you see him?"

Him—Rex. I scan the crowd.

"No," I say. Anxiety inches across my skin. Something feels off—wrong. Did he get caught preparing to escape? Did he leave without Imogene?

I look over at her. Her pale hair catching the overhead lights and creating a soft glow—that along with her white ceremonial dress makes her look even more innocent. But I know that's not entirely true. I know what's hidden under the cotton. Not just the wounds I've given her but the fresh one as well.

People spill through the door part, and Rex's massive frame emerges. I watch as his eyes dart to the stage, from his father's chair to the lack of our own. His jaw ticks, clocking everything in the room.

A bad feeling builds in my gut, that itchy feeling that I would normally rely on my beliefs to combat, but all of that is confused. Muddled by recent events. By my feelings for Imogene and the changes happening in Serendee.

"There he is," Silas says with relief. He turns to Imogene. "How's your wound?"

"Sore," she says, but her pale complexion suggests worse. "I'll be fine."

Is this the compliance we've trained her for? Take the pain and abuse and suffer through it? Ask for more? I know in my heart that it is—and I'm one of the worst.

My confusion turns to nausea. Rex is right. We have to get her out of here.

Rex works his way through the crowd and squeezes between me

and Imogene. I grab his arm. "Did you do it?" I whisper—meaning the money and supplies.

He gives me a short nod. "I tried to catch you before you came in here. This would have been a good cover." He glances around. "Any way we can get out of here before it starts?"

The meetings can go on for hours, but I don't think he's right. Anex would definitely notice their absence. That's confirmed when our leader walks across the stage, eyes going straight to his son and mate.

He's dressed in all black and several of his spiritual wives follow him in, bowing and leading the community to do the same. Margaret stands close, wearing a stomach revealing midriff and a low-slung skirt. Her belly protrudes, the pregnancy obvious. As I follow the motions, touching my forehead in reverence, Rex stands unmoving, staring at Margaret.

"Did you know about this?" he asks. When I don't answer he scowls. He looks to Imogene. "Did you?"

"I just found out tonight," she says. "I didn't get a chance to tell you."

He may forgive her, but it's just another secret I've kept from him, another chink in the bond between us. I want to heal it, solve the rift between us, but he's staring at the stage, at his father, and ultimately, I yank him by the arm after his wives sit at his feet, forcing him to the floor with everyone else.

"I know you're mad, but now isn't the time to get caught up in your anger," I whisper. "We sit through this and then follow your plan. Get Imogene out of here. We'll deal with the rest."

On the stage, Margaret sits on the arm of Anex's chair, positioned for the entire community to see. Her hand strokes the swell of her belly, her bare skin pale and smooth. I wonder if Anex branded her as well.

I realize then that everyone has been removed from the stage, not just us, his other spiritual wives as well. I'm not used to looking at the community from this perspective—on the floor with the others. It's intentional. Everything Anex does is with intention.

"Fuck," Elon mutters, "She's pregnant."

His eyes dart to Rex, waiting for some kind of reaction but it doesn't come. The Rex sitting next to me is the one that is made of stone. Elon looks away, not exactly worried, but he doesn't know about Rex's plan to escape tonight. Or Anex's plans to move Imogene to the childcare center—to take over her Corrections. There are so many changes happening but none compare to what Anex's brought us here for.

"Good morning," Anex says, raising his hand to tug at the short beard on his chin. "Thank you for setting aside your business and work and obligations in order to bask in the glory of The Way." He grins. "I dislike distracting you from the work of the community—it requires many hands and much diligence to keep our Utopia running, but the words that have come to me... well, they can't be held back any longer."

He reaches out and places a hand on Margaret's belly. "As you can see my mate is carrying my child." A series of shouts fill the room, claps and cheers of congratulations. I glance at Rex and see his skin has turned pale. "Thank you. Thank you so much." He holds his hands in a manner to calm and quiet the crowed.

"Becoming a father for the second time, has spurred something in me. The desire to usher Serendee into a new phase. A new birth, as it would seem. I'm sure you've all noticed the construction down on the south field. It's no secret that we're building a childcare center, a place for the infants and toddlers of Serendee to be blessed with the way from the very beginning. It's not just a place of nurturing and care. It will be a birthing center, with midwives and doulas. It will be a place where the women of Serendee can bond over their young, their bodies and practice of The Way and raising devoted children. It will be the finest addition to the community, the one that will lead us into the future, and the first child to be born there, will be my own."

He pauses, and Margaret nods at the wives on the floor, the signal for them to clap, praising Anex for his decision. Next to me Rex mutters, "What the fuck?"

"But I didn't just call you here to spread the good." The room stills at that. "There are some challenges we've been facing. I've been shielding you from this for as long as I could—trying my best to protect the community from Indulgent, Regressive behavior of those that live among us—but that is no longer possible. Not when the people committing the largest indiscretions are part of our leadership and have used their positions to undermine The Way."

Hushed murmurs ripple through those around us, and despite the claustrophobic heat in the room, the hair on the back of my neck stands on end and an uneasy chill climbs my spine.

"It is rare for me to handle something like this so publicly. I prefer smaller, more intimate, meetings when a member of our community has gone astray. But this..." he trails off, his eyes gliding over the crowd, like any one of us could be the offender, "this is too personal. I need witnesses. What better than the whole of Serendee?" His arms lift and he holds up his hands. "Because, brothers and sisters, what has transpired in our quaint, private utopia is blasphemy against the entire community. A mark against everything we do and everything we are."

"What the fuck is he going on about?" Elon whispers. Rex shakes his head, his eyes focused squarely on his father. I see the way his fingers ball into a tight fist. The restraint he uses just to be in Anex's presence.

"We're careful," Anex continues. "So careful about who we allow into Serendee. As you know there is a process, a way to weed out the unworthy and undedicated. Because of that the people we invite into our world help it to flourish and grow." His lips form a thin line. "But sometimes it's not the new blooms that cause the problems. It's the roots, the foundation, which, over the years, without proper attention, rots. It becomes unstable." His eyes flick to our section. "Toxic. My hope is that with early guidance the childcare center will eliminate this problem, but that's the future. Not the presence. To keep our community strong, we must purge the diseased parts and nurture what remains."

The room has grown painfully quiet as we cling to his every

word. As fear builds in our hearts. I can sense the shift in the room. The questions in everyone's minds. *Who. Who is he talking about?*

Anex is never one to leave his followers wanting.

"I need the following people to stand." He clears his throat, eyes flicking down. "Elon, Silas, Levi."

My movements are instinctive. I stand on command, following his words like he has me connected to puppet strings. Elon and Silas do the same and when I steal a look, their expressions are blank. I have no idea what they're thinking. Will he have us remove the offender? Is he separating us from Rex and Imogene before he focuses his attention on them?

"Boys," he says, and my eyes snap to his. "I raised you like my own. I provided you with education, access, skills, and positions of leadership." His eyebrow raises. "And what have you done in return?"

None of us speak. Not even Elon, who I assume is one second from unleashing. What have we given? Our lives. Our souls. Our everything.

I'm not stupid enough to answer. Either are they.

Anex shifts his gaze to Margaret and holds out his hand. She dips her fingers into the collar of her blouse, deep into the crevasse of her swollen breasts, and pulls out a square of paper.

"This is a testimony brought to me from one of our members." He slowly unfolds the paper and takes a long moment to read over the contents. When he looks up, his eyes go directly to Imogene. "Please stand, Imogene."

She quickly gets to her feet, fighting to hide the grimace of pain. Her awkward movements make her trip, stepping on the long hem of her dress. Silas' hand shoots out to catch her. "Careful," he says quietly.

She nods and regains composure, but nothing feels right.

Once she's on her feet, Anex says, "Come stand next to me."

"You don't have to," Rex says, grabbing her wrist.

"Yes, I do," Imogene replies, easing herself from his grip.

Anex, all of us, watch as Imogene walks to the staircase and climbs them. No one else can see the way her nose wrinkles in pain from every step. How the brand sends a jolt of pain through her. I can tell. *We* can tell. All I want to do is chase after her, drag her away from this place—this moment—but she's stronger than I am, crossing the stage and moving next to him.

She bows and honors him again. Thick bile rises to the back of my throat when he speaks, "As you all know, I gave my son and Order this spring, to the lovely Imogene."

She searches for Rex in the crowd and smiles when she finds him. It lights up her entire face, although there's no mistaking the fear in her eyes.

"It was a risky move," Anex says. "The daughter of a Regressive with a powerful man like my son." Rex remains on the floor now. The only one of the five of us. There's no doubt it's with intention. "But my son requested this female and I felt inclined to give him what he wanted. He is the heir, after all." My muscles tighten with every word, and I fight the urge to run up there and pluck her off the stage. "I gave her every opportunity. Access to my wives, invitations to select groups, leeway on the rule surrounding secular society, because of my son's business outside of Serendee." Imogene's face reddens and her fingers twist in the fabric of her dress. "Unfortunately, as I feared, she's like her mother. A betrayer."

Rex bolts to his feet and propelled by rage, pushes past us, rushing to the base of the stage. "She's my mate," he hisses at his father. "Not a betrayer or Regressive."

"Oh, dear boy, you let the allure of what lies between her legs trick you." Anex holds up the paper. "This is a confession—in her own handwriting, isn't that true, Imogene?"

He shows the paper to her and although you can feel the hesitation in her movements, she nods and says, "Yes."

"Good girl," he says, but his tone is flat. Hard. "I'll read the confession to you now, so that you understand the decision I've had to make." He clears his throat. "*I have spent the days since my Ordering in an intimate relationship with my mate's best friends. I've used them to explore my sexuality—to understand Rex's needs and desires.'"* A small curve tugs at Anex's mouth. I don't dare look around me to see the reactions of the other people in the room. My stomach churns. I knew Imogene was forced to tell secrets but this will ruin all of us, and it seems Anex has no plans of stopping. *"'I know it's wrong to be with other men but—'"*

With a roar, Rex leaps up the stage, lunging at his father. "You did this!" he shouts. "You did this to her! You gave her to my friends. Encouraged them to play with her—break her in."

Anex steps out of the way, but his son is too big, too fast, *too angry*, and tackles him to the ground. It only takes a moment before he has his father pinned. Elon is on the stage within a second, standing over the two men. He grabs the paper from Anex's hand and shreds it, tossing the pieces to the ground like confetti.

"Elon!" Silas shouts. Their eyes meet and he jerks his head to the side. It's too late. Anex's guards, heavily armed, charge at the two of them. The room falls into chaos, shouts and screams. The wives fleeing from the stage. Black automatic weapons point and aim. "Get down! Get down! Get down or I'll blow your fucking head off!"

The nose of a rifle presses into Rex's back and he reluctantly releases his father. He lays flat on his stomach, and holds his hands up in an uneasy surrender. Next to him, Elon is shoved to his knees, arms jerked back by the guards, and he's restrained. Neither Silas nor I have moved, but two guards stand by each of us, weapons poised. Anex jerks his head and the guards next to me and Silas, nudge us toward the stairs. Bright lights shine in my eyes as I step on the stage, the audience shrouded in the shadows. The guards stop us by the edge and Elon joins us by force. Rex is still on his stomach, eyes trained on Imogene.

She stands alone on the stage, frozen other than tears streaking down her face, watching in fear. The urge to go to her, to take her hand and run, is strong, but it's nothing compared to the dark sensation in my chest. The one that tells us that we're trapped.

There's no getting out of this.

I wait for Anex to tell the members to leave. To go home while he deals with us, but he stands, giving the signal for quiet. The room falls into a nervous hush, although all I can hear is my heart pounding and the taste of bile in the back of my throat.

"As you see," he says, "I've allowed too much leniency in my son's house. I've allowed too much autonomy between Rex and the boys I called my sons. The young men I placed in my inner circle. There has been too much freedom between the outside world and our community. They've grown weak and Indulgent." He wipes a drop of blood from his mouth where Rex got in a solid hit. He looks down at me and Silas, then over to Elon. "The three of you are no longer welcome in Serendee."

"What?" Imogene cries. She's not the only one, the people around me surge with panic. "You can't—"

"I can and I will!" Anex shouts, the volume of his voice unusual. He's always calm and collected, but today he's rattled. The fight, the letter, using his guards. It's a side of Anex I knew existed, but in private, not public. "This is not open for discussion. You are no longer members of this community. You may not have contact with anyone that lives inside these walls." He looks into the crowd. "Any communication with the Regressive will be banished as well."

Banished.

I understand the word, but in all my time of working with Anex, of being one of his instructors has this only been an option. He Re-educates. He Enlightens. He pushes people to Be Better... but Banishment?

Me?

I've only done what he's asked of me. Followed his directions. I've only ever given my life to this community and our leader. I look over to Silas, who has given just as much, if not more. His face has paled and his body trembles. Elon has retreated into himself, expression blank, eyes cold. He may not look panicked, but I know he is. This is all we've known. It's our home, our family, our community.

I vaguely take in that he's dismissed the room, the residents quietly making their way out the door. They must be confused. *I'm* confused, and once the audience leaves I take a deep breath, and say, "Anex—"

"Do not speak," he snaps, voice low, "not if you want to make it outside these walls without a bullet in the back of your head."

"You did this," Rex shouts as the guards lift him from the ground. "You told them to train my mate. You encouraged it. She never sought this out."

"Did I?" he asks, his tone innocent. "Imogene confessed to her Indulgences. Those were her words, not mine."

"That confession is gone," Elon says. "I tore it up."

Anex laughs and tilts his head to the rafters where a red light blinks menacingly. "If you think I don't have backed up evidence, you truly do not understand me."

That's the thing. I don't understand. This is not the man I loved and respected. He's something dark and nefarious.

"Why are you doing this?" I ask. "Why are you destroying us?"

He walks over and stands before me. He reaches out and I flinch, but he just rests his hand on my shoulder. "Levi, you have been loyal and true, and I tried to give you the opportunity to change with us, but you declined my offer." He grins. "Your response was Indulgent. Selfish. And there's one thing I've learned during my time building this community, it's that if you are not going to fulfill the needs of this community, then Serendee no longer has a place for you. That goes for all of you."

"You don't have a place for us?" I ask. "What does that mean?"

"It means you've become an obstacle to what I want and it's time for you to leave."

"What you want?" Silas asks. "What do you want?"

Anex's gaze swings to Imogene. "Her."

I'm shocked he says it. I think everyone is, but Rex who shouts, "What did you say?"

Anex removes his hand from my shoulder and turns to face his son.

"I know you think you're the one that discovered this little lamb?" He chuckles. "Yes, I know your pet name for her. It's fitting.

I've had my eye on her for a long time—first to make sure she didn't inherit any of her mother's Regressive traits. But as I waited on her to work her way through the Domum, as she came of age, I saw the wild beauty of this precious female." He walks over to Imogene. He touches her cheek, and a shudder rolls down her spine. "I was ready to set her aside, train her for myself, but then you requested her for the Ordering. It pained me, but I figured it was a passing whim. I know the kind of women you like, Rex. The slutty whores of the secular world. I understand—I find them appealing, too—but I figured you'd break her in and cast her aside and if you didn't..."

"You'd have my friends do it."

"Exactly." Anex tucks a loose piece of hair behind Imogene's ear. "At first it worked. You hated her, hurt her, happily handing her over to your friends, who," he looks over at us, "taught her well. Easing her morals. Heightening her desires." His eyes land on mine. "Pushing her to her limits."

"We didn't train her for Rex," Silas says, the pieces clicking into place, "we trained her for *you*."

"You, along with Margaret, and a few other well positioned members of the community. Last night, when she took my brand, things solidified. But really, you did an outstanding job preparing her for this day." He turns away from Imogene. "Unfortunately, I haven't been as satisfied with your other work. The run-in with Jeb was a setback. The refusal to adjust to our new product—"

"You mean sex trafficking," Elon says.

"See... this is the problem. You seem to think that this is a democracy. That you get an opinion in how things operate—how I operate." He walks over to one of the guards and yanks the gun out of his hand, lowering it and pressing the barrel under Elon's chin. "This is a dictatorship and I'm the one in charge. You do as I say, or you suffer the consequences."

"Like being banished," Elon says, ignoring the press of the gun.

"Only two of you are truly being banished," he says, lowering the gun and turning to Silas. "Since Elon decided to destroy my new venture, you'll be the one to explore the feasibility of this trade."

The reality of his statement hits hard. Exploring. Does that mean manage or work. Is he going to traffic Silas or force Silas into trafficking members of the community? It doesn't matter. Either will be enough to destroy him.

"And Rex." He turns to his son. "You're my son. You'll remain here. Frankly, you know too much and are too easy of a target for my enemies. You'll enter re-education training."

"Fuck you and your deranged mind games," Rex growls. "You don't control me and your reeducation is bullshit."

"See?" Anex says with a sigh. "That's the kind of attitude we need to work on. Don't worry. I've been honing my methods."

He nods at one of the guards. He walks over and without warning, shocks Rex with a taser, sending a jolt of energy through his muscular frame.

"Rex!" Imogene cries, watching her mate's body spasm with the shock. "He's your son! What's wrong with you?"

"Nothing, dear girl. I'm just trying to keep my family—my newly upgraded family together." He shifts his gaze to me. "Levi."

"Yes?" A desperate, last flicker of hope fills my chest. It's shameful and corrupt, but it's all I know. This is all I know. "I shouldn't have said no to your offer. I'll take it. Do whatever you want—"

"You and Elon will leave Serendee tonight." His tone is cold and authoritative. "If you attempt to return or contact anyone inside the walls, you'll be shot on sight."

My stomach drops, but there's no time to process it before strong hands grab me from behind. I look to Rex, then Imogene. Both seem frozen. Numb. The same sensation spreads through my limbs.

"Take them," Anex says, waving them off. "I never want to see your faces again."

He waves his hand and the guards snap into action, dragging us toward the side entrance. No one goes easily but the fight isn't fair.

The weapons they have are greater than any resistance we can put forth.

Elon and I are pulled one direction. Silas and Rex another, and before he goes out of view I hear Rex shout, "What about my mate? What are you doing with her?"

"Ah, the Little Lamb," Anex says, nodding at the guard to bring her close to him. She fights, but it's pointless, the guard too strong. His fingers grip her chin, forcing her to look at him. All traces of respect and honor for the man are gone—it's replaced with fear and anger. "I've already told you about your new position. You'll work and live at the childcare center. While you take care of my wife and her unborn child, she'll teach you how to be a proper spiritual wife. How to cater to my needs and demands."

"I won't," she spits out.

His hand shoots down and he drags up the hem of her skirt, revealing the cotton of her undergarments. He hooks a thumb in the top and drags it down, exposing the angry brand. "You agreed to this. You handed yourself over." He loosens his grip, allowing the skirt to fall. His voice softens. "You've spent your whole life waiting for this moment—for true acceptance. Well, the day has come. From now on you'll have the most important job in Serendee." He kisses her forehead. "To fulfill each and every one of my needs and desires."

Horror cascades down her face, recoiling through her body. Anex jerks his head, and the guards descend, pulling all of us in a different directions. I open my mouth and shout, "Anex! Please!" but the sound is muffled when a hood is yanked over my head. The last thing I hear is Rex's voice echoing off the high walls, but it's followed with the sound of electricity crackling.

The barrel of a gun leads me down the stairs—away from my family, my friends, my leader—and Imogene. The girl that changed me in ways I'm only realizing now.

I'm thrust toward a new life.

A life away from Serendee.

AFTERWORD

Book three of The Cult of Serenade: Indulgent is on pre-order on Amazon.

~

Thank you for reading Regressive. Y'all know cults are my jam and digging into the psyche of these people is my playground. Big thanks to everyone who picked up this quirky series and loved it. I appreciate it so much. Special thanks to Lisa, Nikki, & Jennifer for the beta reads and helping me push through some spots! I also looove all the readers in my arc group! So fast and quick to find my nightmare of missing words and spaces.

Angel

~

If you enjoy dark romance you may like my new series, Hunted by My Stepbrothers: Family Confessions. This series was developed for Kindle Vella, and is a dark, forbidden, serial killer romance (yes,

I said those words haha) It's fast paced and completely over the top! Book one is available on Amazon now. Book 2 will be released in September 2022.

For a tease check out the first chapter below:

Hunted by My Stepbrothers
Angel Lawson & AK Rose

Thump.

They're at it again. The noise. The walking. The muffled goddamn voices above my room. I thought by now they'd be better at hiding what they do. They don't care. Of course they don't care. I mean, why would they? It's not like they give a shit about me, laying underneath their bedroom.

If the Davenport brothers have proven anything, it's that they don't give a shit about me.

I shift and turn, the house humid from the afternoon storm, hating the way my top sticks to my skin.

God, I didn't want to be back here, in this house... in this family. Four years away at school and it's like nothing has changed. A family of strangers, except for mom. Mom, who always does whatever Montie, my stepfather, wants.

Thump.

I flinch at the sound. I can't sleep, not with them on the floor above or the damn southern sweltering heat. *Bang.* The shutter smacks against the window, making me flinch. Jesus, this house. I never know what's causing the creaks and groans.

Is it the hundred-and-fifty-year-old rafters or the ancient oak tree out front, draped in ghostly Spanish moss? The house has been in Monte's family for generations and no matter how clean my mother or the housekeepers keep it, the scent of musty air clings to everything that resides inside.

I forgot how sticky the night breeze feels, nothing like the cooler weather up north. There, the heat of summer is still a few weeks away. Lightning flashes in the distance, the soft white lighting up my bedroom before it flickers and fades away. Thunder follows with a low creeping rumble.

No, not thunder. My senses sharpen at the sound. I lift my head from the pillow, listening. A car. *Their car.* The deep sound of the engine echoing off the trees. I rise from the bed, sliding my feet from under the sheets. The sounds are followed by the slam of a car door. One, two... only two tonight. For now, at least. They tend to roam in a pack, or at least they used to.

At the window, I adjust the curtain and lift my gaze, searching for the lick of cool air as headlights flare on the street far below my window.

I skim my hand against my breast. My fingers brushing my nipples, tight, puckered, aching with my impending period. The flimsy negligee is more lace than satin. Pink with matching panties. It's all I can stand to wear at night in this heat. The family is rich, *filthy* rich, so why the hell don't they have AC?

"It would detract from the historical preservation of Davenport Manor if we added air conditioning," I can hear Monte explain. God forbid we offend the preservation society for a little bit of comfort and sanity.

Down on the driveway, the car pulls out, headlights lighting the way until they are gone.

I breathe a sigh of relief knowing they're gone. I wouldn't be here now if it wasn't for the interview at the Gazette in the morning. I should've known better than to get a degree in a dying field–print journalism. But it's my passion. To my dismay, Monte pulled a few strings and got me the interview with one of his friends. Nepotism isn't the way I want to make it in the business–but my mother never would've let me live it down if I'd declined such a kind gesture from my stepfather. So here I am, back in Davenport Manor, sticky with sweat and listening to my stepbrothers bang around upstairs all night.

Some things never change.

I hate being here while they're home, especially when mom and Monte are gone. They'd already scheduled their trip when I announced I was coming back home to look for a job. I got home two days ago and have managed to avoid the boys the whole time.

Boys.

They're men, now. Twenty-five and twenty-four.

Thump.

I flinch and look at the ceiling. Lightning flickers again, this time brighter, bolder, carrying with it the faint scent of ozone on the thick air. I swallow more than suck, taking in that bitter scent and licking my lips, tasting salt and sweat.

Thump.

It's followed by another sound this time. Low and deep. A groan.

My heart thumps, muffling the sound as I swallow and glance at the window, searching the place where the car was parked. Still gone. Still empty... but that sound.

Moan...

"What the fuck?" I whisper, again staring at the ceiling.

The sounds were always the same; the thud of footsteps. The creak of the old hardwood floors. They did it on purpose; I was sure of it, just to piss me off. They were always the same, *my stepbrothers.* Moody. Brooding. Secretive.

Oliver and Jack Davenport.

Stay the fuck out of our way.

The words resound in my head. It was the first interaction we ever had. Sure made a lasting impression. The only one that counted, really. After that was a long succession of doors being slammed in my face and hostile glares from Jack, mostly. He's the oldest–the scariest. The main asshole who didn't care about getting a new little sister when our parents married. Oliver wasn't much better, although, sometimes, when we were alone, he'd talk to me, making me feel special. But then, just as fast, Jack would appear and whatever kindness he showed me would vanish quick as a whisper.

Mom would say they were just dealing with their own emotions about losing their mother. They were just hormonal teenage boys. Well, I was fourteen, with raging hormones of my own.

"Help..."

The voice is louder, stronger, and I stumble back, slamming my hand against my chest. I wait a beat, then walk to the door, cracking it open. Listening, certain I'd heard wrong, I—

"Help... someone help me..."

I yank the door shut; the latch echoing in the quiet house, and press my back against the wood.

Fuck. This is my fault. I'd always had nightmares here. Always had the wildest imagination.

"Please..."

The word hit me like ice in my veins. I stop, panic roaring inside me as I muster up the courage to open the door again. "I heard wrong. I heard wrong. I heard—" I tell myself, but I know that I didn't hear anything wrong. I'm not crazy, I promise myself as I push the door open wider, glancing along the balustrade to the stairs. I step into the dark hallway. Dark and silent and old. My bare feet creak on the hardwoods as I near the stairs. "Mom?"

Silence answers, wind whistles through the cracks in the downstairs windows. I step out further, gripping the banister and move to the first step. "Mont?"

There was nothing. Nothing. My mind was playing tricks. I knew I shouldn't have had that last glass of wine—

"Anyone... please..."

I jerk, wrenching my gaze up to the stairs. The voice came from the third floor.

The one place I was forbidden to go in the house. A place where bad things happen. But that was years ago, and before I heard someone crying for help. I move without thinking, rounding the landing, and climb.

Stay the fuck out of our way.

"Stay the fuck out," I repeat, climbing the first stair and then the next. The house is hulking and mammoth. Character, that's what mom called it. The damn thing just creeped me out.

When mom and I moved into this house, it was my fourteenth birthday. Even then I was scared, weirded out by the size and musty smell. But all mom saw was a future. One where we weren't poor, and she was no longer a widow and single mother.

I try not to think about that as I climb the stairs. The third floor was off limits to everyone, including the housekeeper. I ignore the rules put in place all those years ago. I'm no longer a scrawny teenager intimidated by my stepbrothers and their friends.

"Help..."

Christ, the voice is louder the higher I go. "Hello?" I call out, inching to the top of the stairs. I scan the landing and squint, searching for the murky outline of the bedroom doors. My heart pounds remembering the only time I came this far into their territory. I'd paid for the violation. I clear my throat. "Jack? Oliver?"

My voice trails into a whisper as I quietly make my way to the first door.

Creak.

My pulse jumps with sound. Heart hammers, I jerk my gaze over my shoulder. But there's no one there. Just this house. "This creepy fucking house. I swear I'm gonna die of a goddamn heart attack in this place." I say it out loud, like I can force myself to reason. I turn back, moving to the doorway and grip the handle.

My nightie sticks against my thighs, pulling taut as I turn and ease open the door, inch-by-inch. "If this is some kind of twisted joke, I swear I'll scream so loud the entire neighborhood will hear." My voice betrays me. It's nothing but a croak.

I can't hear a thing over the booming of my heart. Still, I force myself to move, stepping inside the bedroom. The scent of something dark and sultry hit me. I recognize the scent, the man it belongs to, and inhale deep...

Only that's a mistake. Under the seductive scent of something erotic and manly, a sickening, copper smell hits my nostrils... *blood.*

I reach out, my fingers smacking against the doorframe, before I reach along the wall, searching. *Click.* I hit the switch, and the room floods with a dull, yellow light, leaving me to turn my head. I freeze.

"Help me." The voice comes from a man and for a second I don't understand what I'm seeing...

No.

God...

It doesn't just smell like blood, it's there. Everywhere. The guy lies on his side on the ground. His hands tied behind his back, curled up, with his ankles strapped together by tape. A chair turned over behind him. There's blood *everywhere*, weeping from his head, dripping into his eyes. He looks up at me.

"Jesus." I glance around, trying to absorb what has become of Jack's bedroom. There's a bench along the wall. Spread across the surface are dozens of knives. Several coated in the sticky residue of blood. "What is this? Who are you?"

"Untie me." The guy pleads and closes his eyes. "Please, just untie me and let me go."

"I'm c-calling the cops," I stutter, moving back to the safety of the hallway.

"No." He shakes his head, his voice slurring. "Just let me go. I promise not to say anything. I promise you'll never hear from me again. *I just need to get out of here before they come back.*"

I step forward, glancing at those knives once more, and then kneel down. But I don't touch him. He's filthy, muddy, and God, bloody. I glance at the tape wrapped tight around his jeans and then drift my gaze up to his arms cinched around his back.

"The key." He urges, holding my eye. "You need to find the key."

"Key?"

"For the handcuffs."

Oh, shit. I nod. "Okay. Okay, I can do this," I say, more to myself than him. I rise and scan the bedroom, trying to figure out where they'd put the key. I spot a messy desk, although it was more than that, more like one of those investigation rooms the cops use on Murderers Most Wanted. A large map hangs over the desk, string zig-zags between photographs and hand-written notes. "Oh fuck, oh fuck," I chant to myself. This is bad. So fucking bad.

I search the desk, fumbling through drawers and under stacks of paper, but there's no key. I turn, spotting a duffle bag splayed open on his bed. I stumble forward and hesitate, not wanting to touch the damn thing.

"Hurry," the guy bleeding out on my stepbrother's bedroom floor whispers. *His anxiety is contagious.*

"I'm trying," I snap, then take a deep breath. It's just a normal day, right? Just a goddamn normal day in this hellhole.

I yank open the bag and rifle through the contents. Black masks. Black tape. Two rolls of it, because of course, I mean why wouldn't you have plenty, right? I yank through the stuff, touching cold steel before tearing my hand away.

I can't do this.

I can't...

Get your shit together, Katie! He's right. They'll be back soon.

Desperation kicks hard. I step forward, grabbing the handle of the bag and upend the contents on the bed. Metal glints underneath the mess. I shove rolls of plastic bags aside and grab the set of two tiny keys.

"Yes! That's it!" the guy shouts, as I turn and hurry toward him.

"I'm going to get you out of here." I kneel, filled with purpose, and reach for his hands. "And then we'll call the police."

He rolls onto me, his breath warm against my thigh. I should be more aware of how high my nightie rides, and how exposed I am, but I push that aside. This isn't the time to be self-conscious. Not when I'm saving someone's life.

My fingers tremble as I shove the key into the lock.

Creak.

The house shifts, only this time I don't care. I *can't* care. The lock gives a *click,* and the cuffs release, allowing his hands to fall. He rips the tape off from around his ankles, and I exhale in relief.

"I left my phone in my room, just let me go—" my words are cut short when I feel the tight grip of his fingers around my throat.

"Stupid bitch." He snarls, squeezing tighter. He isn't the helpless victim anymore. The glint in his eye, the curl of his lip, it says everything. He's not the prey, he's a predator.

Panic roars, and a scream is trapped by his fingers as he grips tight.

"Aren't you a doll?" he laughs. "Coming up here to save me like a good little bitch. It's going to be fun to cut you up." His breath is rancid and hot. "Right after I rip that pretty nightie off and stuff it in your mouth so no one will hear your screams while I fuck your last breath out of you."

His anger and rage are palpable. It tremors through his blood slicked fingertips. I see a flash of my future, my stepbrothers returning to find me exactly how he described. Would they laugh at stupid Kate for getting herself into such a mess?

His gaze jerks over my shoulder, and he stills.

The flash of silver glints beside me as a knife carves through the air and buries into the center of his throat. Then, with one savage jerk, his throat tears open. Blood shoots out, splashing my chest just like the warm, sultry night air. A scream rips free, shrill, *terrifying,* before something clamps across my mouth, cutting off the sound.

Warm leather flattens against my lips. A heavy breath near my ear. I'm hauled to my feet, pushed backwards and slammed against the wall. My head cracks with the impact, detonating white stars behind my eyes as I stare into the chilling eyes of a murderer.

"Shouldn't have come up here, little sister." Jack sucks in a hard breath and glances over his shoulder. The man chokes and sputters. His hands flap wildly against the floor as he bleeds out. Then my stepbrother turns that depraved glare my way. "Should've stayed the hell out of our way, like I told you to."

My heart booms. Terror screaming inside me as he lowers his gaze to the blood that drips down my breasts, adhering the thin fabric of my top against my chest. "The question is, Katie. What the fuck do we do with you now?"

Find Hunted Here!

www.ingramcontent.com/pod-product-compliance
Lightning Source LLC
Chambersburg PA
CBHW020033310726
48970CB00007B/2232